LOYALTIES

LOYALTIES

DELPHINE DE VIGAN

*Translated from the French
by George Miller*

BLOOMSBURY PUBLISHING
LONDON · OXFORD · NEW YORK · NEW DELHI · SYDNEY

BLOOMSBURY PUBLISHING
Bloomsbury Publishing Plc
50 Bedford Square, London, WC1B 3DP, UK

BLOOMSBURY, BLOOMSBURY PUBLISHING and the Diana logo are
trademarks of Bloomsbury Publishing Plc

First published in Great Britain 2019

A catalogue record for this book is available from the British Library

ISBN: HB: 978-1-5266-0198-8; TPB: 978-1-5266-0199-5; EBOOK: 978-1-5266-0200-8

2 4 6 8 10 9 7 5 3 1

Typeset by Integra Software Services Pvt. Ltd.
Printed and bound in Great Britain by CPI Group (UK) Ltd, Croydon CR0 4YY

To find out more about our authors and books visit www.bloomsbury.com and
sign up for our newsletters

Loyalties.

They're invisible ties that bind us to others – to the dead as well as the living. They're promises we've murmured but whose echo we don't hear, silent fidelities. They're contracts we make, mostly with ourselves, passwords acknowledged though unheard, debts we harbour in the folds of our memories.

They're the rules of childhood dormant within our bodies, the values in whose name we stand up straight, the foundations that enable us to resist, the illegible principles that eat away at us and confine us. Our wings and our fetters.

They're the springboards from which our strength takes flight and the trenches in which we bury our dreams.

HÉLÈNE

I thought the kid was being abused. I had this thought very quickly, maybe not in the first few days, but not long after the school year began. There was something about the way he acted, how he looked away. I recognise that. I know it by heart. A way of blending into the background, of letting the light pass through you. Except with me that doesn't work. I was hit when I was a child and I hid the marks right to the end, so I'm not taken in. I say 'the kid' because really you should see boys at that age, with their hair as fine as girls', their high, fluting voices and the sense of uncertainty that clings to their movements. You should see them look amazed with their eyes out on stalks, or getting told off with their hands clasped tight behind their backs, their lips quivering, as though butter wouldn't melt in their mouths. And yet there's no doubt that this is the age when they start to do really stupid things.

A few weeks into the new school year I requested an appointment with the Head about Théo Lubin. I had to go through it a few times. No, there were no marks and he hadn't confided in me. It was something to do with his attitude, as though he was closed up, a particular way of avoiding attention. Mr Nemours laughed at first: avoiding attention? Wasn't that true of half the class? Yes, of course I knew what he meant: the way they have of shrinking in their seats to avoid being asked a question, of rummaging in their bags or suddenly becoming absorbed in looking at their desks as if it were a matter of life or death. I can recognise that sort without even needing to look up. But this was completely different. I asked what we knew about the student and his family. We should be able to find some information in the file, comments, a previous warning sign. The Head carefully went through the comments on his reports. Several teachers had indeed noted how quiet he was last year, but that was all. He read them out: 'highly introverted pupil', 'needs to participate in class', 'good marks, but too quiet', and so on. The parents are separated, they have joint custody, all the usual stuff. The Head asked me if Théo was friends with any other boys in his class and I had to admit he was. They're always huddled together, the pair of them. They're lucky to have found each other. Same angelic face, same colour of hair, same clear complexion. You'd think they were twins. I watch them from the window when they're in the playground. They form a single entity – wild, a sort of jellyfish that suddenly retracts when approached, then expands again when the danger's past. The rare times I see Théo smile are when he's with Mathis Guillaume, and no adult has breached their security perimeter.

The only thing that caught the Head's attention was the nurse's report from the end of last year. This report wasn't in the main file. It was Frédéric who suggested I went to see the nurse, just in case. In late May Théo had asked to be excused. He said he had a headache. The nurse mentioned he'd had an evasive attitude and confused symptoms. She'd noted that his eyes were red. Théo had told her that it took him a long time to get to sleep and sometimes he lay awake most of the night. At the foot of the page she'd written 'delicate student' and underlined it three times. Then she probably closed the file and put it back in the cabinet. She'd left the school, so I couldn't talk to her.

But for this file, I'd never have succeeded in getting Théo called in to see the new nurse.

I talked to Frédéric about it and he seemed concerned. He told me I shouldn't take it all so much to heart. He thought I'd seemed tired for a while: 'on a knife edge' were the words he used, and that immediately made me think of the knife my father had kept in the kitchen drawer, which anyone could have found there, a flick knife. He'd play with the security catch, mechanically, over and over, to calm his nerves.

THÉO

It's a wave of heat he can't describe. It burns and sets him alight. It hurts, but it's also comforting, a moment that lasts just a few seconds and must have a name, but he doesn't know it, a chemical name, physiological, which could convey its strength and intensity, a word that sounds something like 'combustion' or 'explosion' or 'detonation'. He's twelve and a half and if he answered the questions that adults ask him honestly – 'What job would you like to do?', 'What are you passionate about?', 'What do you want to do in life?' – if he weren't afraid that his last remaining supports would immediately collapse, he'd unhesitatingly reply: 'I like the feeling of alcohol in my body.' First in his mouth, that moment when his throat welcomes the liquid, and then those fractions of a second as the warmth goes down into his stomach. He could trace its route with his finger. He loves the moist wave that caresses the back of his neck and spreads through his limbs like an anaesthetic.

He gulps and coughs several times. Mathis is sitting opposite him, watching and laughing. Théo thinks of the dragon in the picture book that his mother used to read to him when he was little, with its huge body, knife-slit eyes and open jaws that revealed fangs far sharper than the most vicious dog's. He wishes he were that huge creature with webbed feet, able to set fire to everything. He takes a deep breath, then another swig from the bottle. When he lets the alcohol numb him, when he tries to visualise where it goes, he imagines one of the diagrams Ms Destrée hands out in class on which they have to name each part: 'Show the journey of the apple and indicate which organs are involved in digestion.' He smiles at this image, amused to be twisting it: 'Show the journey of the vodka; colour its trajectory; calculate the time required for the first mouthfuls to reach your blood ...' He laughs to himself and, seeing him laugh, Mathis laughs too.

A few minutes later, something explodes in his brain, like a door being kicked open, a powerful inrush of air and dust, and the image that comes into his mind is of the swing doors of a saloon in the Wild West bursting open. And for an instant he's a cowboy in cowboy boots striding to the bar in the gloom, his spurs making a dull sound as they scrape the floor. And when he leans on the bar to order a whisky, he feels as though everything has been obliterated – the fear and the memories. The owl's talons that are always pressing into his chest have finally released their grip. He closes his eyes. Everything has been washed clean, and everything can begin.

Mathis takes the bottle from his hands and raises it to his own lips. Turn and turn about. The vodka spills out, a transparent trickle runs down his chin. Théo protests: it doesn't count if he spits it out. So Mathis swallows it down and his eyes begin to water. He coughs, puts his hand to his mouth, and for an instant Théo wonders if he's about to throw up, but after a few seconds Mathis can't stop himself laughing even harder. Théo immediately clamps his hand over his mouth to shut him up. Mathis stops laughing.

They hold their breath, keep still and listen for any sounds around them. In the distance they hear the voice of a teacher they can't identify, a droning monologue in which no words are distinguishable.

They're in their hiding place, their safe place. This is their territory. Under the canteen stairs they've discovered this empty space, one square metre almost high enough for them to stand up in. A large cupboard has been put here to block access, but with a bit of agility, they can slide underneath. It all comes down to timing. They have to hide in the toilets until everyone has gone back to class. Then wait a few more minutes until the hall monitor has done the hourly check to make sure no pupils are hanging around the corridors.

Every time they manage to slip under the cupboard, they realise they have just centimetres to spare. In a few months, they won't be able to do it any more.

Mathis passes him the bottle.

After a final swig, Théo runs his tongue over his teeth. He loves the taste of salt and metal that lingers in his mouth for a long time, sometimes for hours.

The distance between index finger and thumb is their way of gauging how much they've drunk. They try to do this several times, without managing to keep their fingers still. They burst out laughing.

They've drunk a lot more than last time.

And the next time, they'll drink even more.

This is their pact, and their secret.

Mathis takes the bottle back, wraps it in paper and slips it into his rucksack.

They each take two sticks of Airwaves mint and liquorice gum. They chew them carefully to release the flavour, moving the gum around their mouths. It's the only kind that conceals the smell. They're waiting for the right moment to re-emerge.

Once they're back on their feet, they feel different. Théo's head is bobbing back and forward imperceptibly.

He's tiptoeing across a liquid carpet with a geometric pattern. He feels as though he's outside his own body, just alongside it, as though he'd left his body but is still holding it by the hand.

School noises barely reach him. They're muted by some invisible, absorbent liquid that's protecting him.

———

One day, he'd like to completely lose consciousness.

Plunge into the dense fabric of drunkenness and allow himself to be covered, buried, for a few hours or forever. He knows that can happen.

HÉLÈNE

I'm watching him without meaning to. I'm aware that my attention keeps going back to him. I force myself to look at the others, one by one, when I'm talking and they're listening, or when they're hunched over their Monday-morning test. It was Monday in fact when I saw him come into class, his face even paler than usual. He looked like a kid who hadn't had a minute's sleep all weekend. His actions were the same as everyone else's – taking off his jacket, pulling out his chair, putting his rucksack on the table, unzipping it and taking out his exercise book – I can't even say that it struck me as slower than usual, nor more jittery, and yet I could tell he was exhausted. At the start of the lesson, I thought he was going to fall asleep, because he's already done that a couple of times since the start of the year.

Later, when I was talking about Théo in the staffroom, Frédéric pointed out, without irony, that that hardly made him unique.

Given the time they waste staring at their screens, if we worried about every pupil who looked tired, we'd spend all our time producing reports. Dark rings round their eyes don't prove anything.

It's irrational, I know.

I've got nothing. Nothing at all. No facts and no proof. Frédéric is trying to stop me worrying so much. And being so impatient. The nurse has said she'll ask to see him and I believe her.

The other evening I tried to explain this oppressive feeling of a countdown I've had for a few days, as if a timer had been activated without our knowledge and precious time was draining away without us being able to hear it, leading us in silent procession towards something ridiculous whose impact we're incapable of imagining.

Frédéric told me again that I looked tired.

He said, 'You're the one who should be resting.'

This morning I went on with the lesson about the digestive system. Théo suddenly sat up, listening with more focused attention than normal. I drew a diagram on the board showing how liquids are absorbed and he copied it down in his exercise book with unusual patience.

At the end of class, I couldn't stop myself keeping him behind. I don't know what had got into me, but I put my hand on his shoulder to get his attention and said, 'Théo, will you stay behind for a minute, please?' Immediately an indignant murmur rippled through the class: what right did I have to detain a pupil without an explicit reason when nothing had happened during the lesson to justify my request? I waited till everyone had gone. Théo still had his head down. I didn't know what to say, but I couldn't back off, so I had to come up with something, a pretext, a question, anything at all. What had I been thinking? When the door finally closed behind the last pupil (Mathis Guillaume, of course), I still had nothing. The silence went on for a few seconds, Théo kept staring at his Nikes. And then he looked up. I think it was the first time he'd looked at me properly, without his eyes darting away. He stared at me but said nothing. I'd never seen such an intense stare from a boy of his age. He didn't look surprised or impatient. It wasn't a questioning look, as though it was completely normal that we should have ended up like this, as though it were all preordained, a foregone conclusion. Equally obvious was the impasse we were in, the impossibility of taking another step forward, of venturing anything. He looked at me as though he'd understood the instinct that made me keep him back, as though he also understood that I couldn't take it any further. He realised exactly what I was feeling.

He knew that I knew, and that I could do nothing for him.

That's what I thought. And that suddenly choked me up.

I don't know how long this went on. The words were scrambled in my head – parents, home, tiredness, sadness, everything OK? – but none of them produced a question I would have allowed myself to ask.

In the end I smiled, I think, and in a voice I didn't recognise, an uncertain voice that didn't belong to me, I heard myself ask, 'Are you with your father or your mother this week?'

He hesitated before answering.

'My father. Well, until this evening.'

He picked up his bag to put over his shoulder, the signal that he was about to go, which I should have let him do some time ago. He headed towards the door.

Just before he left, he turned to me and said, 'But if you want to speak to my parents, it'll be my mother who comes.'

THÉO

After school he hung around outside for ten minutes and then went back to his father's to pick up his things. The curtains hadn't been opened. He just put on the kitchen light to see his way to his bedroom. As he crossed the living room, he heard a strange sound, a sort of intermittent, muffled crackling, as though an insect were trapped somewhere. In the darkness he tried to work out where the noise was coming from and then he realised the radio had been left on since the morning and the volume turned down so that the words could no longer be made out.

Every Friday it's the same drill: he gets everything together, his clothes, shoes, all his books, folders and exercise books, his table tennis bat, his ruler, tracing paper, felt pens, drawing pad. He mustn't forget anything. Every Friday, loaded up like a mule, he migrates from one place to another.

In the metro carriage, people look at him. They're probably afraid that he'll fall or faint, his small body staggering under the weight of all those bags. He bends, but he doesn't weaken. He refuses to sit down.

In the lift, before he lands on the opposite shore, he puts down his load, gives himself time to catch his breath.

This is what he has to do every Friday at more or less the same time: this shift from one world to the other, with no gangway or guide. Two complete worlds, without any common ground.

Eight metro stops away: another culture, other customs, another language. He only has a few minutes to acclimatise.

It's half past six when he opens the door, and his mother is already home.

She's sitting in the kitchen, chopping intriguingly shaped vegetables. He'd like to ask what they're called but now's not the right time.

She looks at him, scrutinises him, scans him silently, her eye a radar. She can't help it. She's suspicious. She hasn't seen him for a week, but there's no hug. It's the imprint of the other that she's looking for, even though she fears it: the trace of the enemy.

She can't bear it that he's come from over there. Théo grasped that very quickly from the air of distrust she displays when he comes back from his father's and the impulse to reject him, which she has trouble hiding.

And anyway, even before she says hello, she generally says 'go and have a shower'.

They won't talk about the days he's spent with his father. It's a black hole in time and space whose very existence will be denied. She won't ask him anything, he knows. She won't ask if he had a good week or if he's OK. She won't ask if he's eaten well, slept well, what he's seen or done. She'll pick up where they left off a week ago, exactly as though nothing has happened, as though nothing *could* have happened. A week of his life struck off the calendar. But for his diary – every day he carefully tears off the perforated corner of the page – he might doubt he'd experienced it.

He'll put the clothes he's wearing in the laundry basket, all of them without exception, separately, sealed in a plastic bag because she refuses to let them come into contact with his other ones. The hot water in the shower will wash away the smell she cannot abide.

In the hours after his return she'll observe him with a hostility she's not even conscious of but he's all too familiar with, that air of interrogation. Because, in her son who is not yet thirteen, she's in relentless pursuit of the gestures, inflections, posture of the man whose name she will no longer utter. Any real or imagined resemblance enrages her and becomes the subject of an immediate riposte, a sickness that has to be eradicated at once. 'Look how you're standing. Don't do that with your hands. Sit back in your seat. Don't slouch. Sit up. You're just like him.'

'Go to your room.'

When she mentions his father, when circumstances force her to refer to the man who was her husband and at whose home he has just spent an entire week, when there's no way around it, she never uses his first name.

She says 'him', 'that bastard', 'that loser'.

When she's talking to her friends on the phone he's 'that shit' or 'that dirty bastard'.

Théo absorbs this, his puny body spattered with words, but she doesn't see it. The words are hurting him; they're an unbearable ultrasound, a feedback loop that only he seems to hear, an inaudible frequency that shreds his brain.

During the night after his return a high-pitched, faraway sound wakes him. A piercing note, a static whistle that comes from inside him. If he clamps his hands over his ears, the sound at first grows louder and then fades. It's called tinnitus. He read about it on a health website. The noise swells up more and more often in the middle of the night. At first he thought it was coming from outside. He'd get up. He'd go into the kitchen, listen to the appliances, the pipes in the bathroom, he'd open the front door. And then he realised.

The noise is in his head. When the noise eventually stops, he can't get back to sleep.

He has just one memory of his parents together.

His mother is sitting on a hard sofa upholstered in a foamy mustard fabric (in fact, he's not sure if he really remembers this sofa. It's possible he's copied the detail of this image from a photo. Ms Destrée taught them that at the beginning of the year; there are things we retain in the memory, others that we transform or manufacture, still others that we appropriate). His mother is sitting stiff and tense, not leaning on the backrest. His father is pacing up and down in front of her like a caged animal. Théo is sitting on the floor or maybe beside his mother, who is not touching him. He has to raise his head to see them. He's a child of four and a bit, the watchful observer of a smouldering war that's about to explode.

Then there are the words his mother says, words that strike him immediately, make him gasp, words that are saved on his hard drive, adult words charged with a meaning he can't grasp but whose power he registers. His mother is looking down, but she's talking to his father when she says, 'You disgust me.'

They've forgotten he's there or else they think he's too young to understand, to remember, but it's precisely because these words contain something he can't grasp, something solid and maybe a little sticky, that he will remember them.

At this moment, neither he nor she can imagine that their son of four years and a few months will have just one memory of them together and this will be it.

———

Théo comes out of the bathroom wearing clean clothes. He thinks about Ms Destrée wanting to know which of his parents he was spending the week with. She'd looked at him in a funny way. When he caught up with Mathis at the school gate, he said, 'That woman's crazy.' But now, thinking back, his forehead flushes with a feeling of shame that spreads to his throat. He's sorry he said that.

His mother is still in the kitchen, half-listening to something on the radio as she finishes making dinner. He asks if he can go on YouTube.

'No.'

He can get on with his homework. He must have work to catch up on.

For the next few hours, maybe even until tomorrow, she's going to make him pay for having set foot on enemy territory, for having been outside her law, her control, for having had fun.

Because she's sure he will have taken full advantage, he'll have done nothing all week but stare at screens, stuffing himself with crisps and Coke and staying up till all hours.

That's what she imagines.

It doesn't matter what she imagines.

Anyway, he's not going to contradict her.

HÉLÈNE

The nurse asked to see Théo this week.

The day after his appointment she suggested we had coffee to talk it over. She came to the staffroom at lunchtime. She related in detail the conversation she'd had with him. She talked to me as though I were unwell, as though someone had warned her I needed to be handled carefully, talked to gently.

She'd begun by telling Théo that several of his teachers were worried about how tired he was. They'd told her he'd fallen asleep in class a couple of times. That he had trouble concentrating.

She wanted to know what was going on, how he was feeling.

He asked if it was me who had told on him.

She said that no one had *told on* him and repeated that several teachers were worried about how tired he seemed and wanted to make sure everything was OK. That was all.

He relaxed a bit.

He admitted he found it very hard to get to sleep, or rather that he was waking up during the night. He said several times that he was not playing on a tablet or games console – or very little. She tried questioning him about his family but got nothing out of him. His mother had a management job in a pharmaceutical company and his father was in IT. The joint custody arrangement dated back to their separation several years ago. She asked him how things were with his parents and he replied without enthusiasm but also without hesitation, 'They're fine.'

She admitted she found him anxious and a little defensive. But not more so than the situation might have caused, given that he was the only pupil in his class she'd asked to see. She asked him if she could listen to his chest on the grounds that lack of sleep sometimes causes growth and development problems, and he didn't object.

There were no marks on his body. Smooth skin, pure, intact. Not so much as a scratch or a scar. His height and weight were slightly below average for his age, but nothing alarming.

She wrote a letter for his mother, which she gave to Théo.

In it she mentioned his drowsiness in class and the need to see a doctor to tackle the insomnia problem.

She told Théo that he could come and see her whenever he liked and suggested he tried to rest a bit during breaks if he felt tired.

She's done her job, I can't deny it. She followed the rules. She promised that she'd stay alert. And she went back to her antiseptic domain, sparkling floor, protected space, sheltered. I stayed in the staffroom. I couldn't get up. I was sitting with my back to the door with a pile of exercise books in front of me and the almost empty plastic cup with coffee I couldn't drink getting cold in the bottom. I told myself: Get up and go home. I'd finished for the day and I could feel the wave swelling, a backwash from the sewer, brackish, stinking waters. The black tide of memory was starting to rise to the surface. First the sounds: the broken fridge, asthmatic snoring, television jingles in the background, laughter, encouragements, applause. And then the images: curtains stained yellow by nicotine, rickety chairs, chipped ornaments.

Nothing seems completely intact in that room, but on the television the Wheel spins and people are having fun. 'First riddle. I'll buy an A; I offer an N.' The Wheel turns again, unpredictable fortune: good luck!

We have our own game too, my father and I, at the same time as the TV. It starts without warning, for no reason, while I'm drawing or doing my homework. The first question rents the air and announces the torture: 'Since you know everything, Hélène, when was the guillotine was invented?'

I'm eight. Eleven. Thirteen. I'm always in the same place, sitting at the kitchen table, hands flat on the oilcloth. My father's home early, he's thinking up a quiz for his daughter. She works hard in class – big deal. She reads books, claims she wants to become a primary school teacher and it's as if she's spitting in the face of her father, who was expelled from school. Since she acts so clever, he's going to ask her some questions to see what she knows.

One wrong answer: a tap on the top of the head. Two wrong answers: a slap.

Three wrong answers and he pushes me off my stool and I fall on the floor.

Four wrong answers and I stay on the ground and he gives me a kick.

'When was Joan of Arc canonised?'

'In which year did Charles Martel win the Battle of Poitiers?'

Sometimes the questions are the same as on the TV game show, sometimes not. The rules keep changing.

I try to concentrate. It's not easy with the noise of *Wheel of Fortune*. The music's so loud. 'You get to play again, Roselyne. Well done. You didn't lose the ball, ha ha! Now you need to work out an expression. OK, listen carefully, Roselyne.' I'm lying on the floor, as always. I'm not allowed to get up. I'm no longer search-ing for answers – I'm waiting for the next blow. 'The correct answer was "pie in the sky", Roselyne, too bad.' I never cry.

The questions no longer make sense and he keeps on kicking me. I try to protect my head. I curl up on the floor and try to avoid the kicks to the stomach that wind me; his boots have hard, round toecaps. My father wears protective footwear, even though he no longer works on the shop floor. 'And you've chosen this sapphire and diamond ring, Roselyne. You'll get that along with its international gemological certificate for a total of nine thousand nine hundred francs. You're taking home some very nice prizes all the same.'

I'm fourteen. I'm lying on the floor when my mother gets back. I may have been unconscious for a few seconds or minutes. When I stand up, there's blood trickling from between my legs, a scarlet snake sliding down my calf seeking refuge in my socks. My mother asks if I have my period and I say no.

A few weeks later I'm in maths class and the pain is clawing at the pit of my stomach. I'm having trouble breathing, it's hard not to groan. The teacher notices I'm not listening. He asks me about what he just said but I can't answer. The walls are spinning faster than the Wheel of Fortune, the floor is pulling me in. I don't even know what the lesson is about. The teacher gets angry and tells me to leave. In the corridor I faint.

In the hospital they diagnose an infected uterus. Not a pretty sight.

I tell them I fell off a bike rack onto a concrete kerb. I don't know yet that I won't be able to have children.

I'm seventeen. I've passed my bac and I'm leaving. My father has just died of cancer. His decline lasted two years, two years of truce with no games and no kicks, just the occasional swipe when I passed within range.

Now it was my father's turn to be on the floor. My mother looked after him right to the end.

I'm seventeen. I'm going to study. I'm going to become a teacher. I'm not going to forget any of it.

CÉCILE

I talk to myself. At home when I'm alone and in the street when I'm sure no one can see me. Yes, I talk to myself, but it would be more accurate to say that one part of me talks to the other. I say, 'You'll get there,' 'You did it!' or 'You can't go on like this.' Those are examples. I tried to explain this to Dr Felsenberg when I met him a few weeks ago, this thing about there being two parts of me. The very first time. He thought it was worth clarifying. OK. So: one part of me, which is dynamic and which I would call positive, talks to the other part. My weak part. To keep it simple, let's call it the problem part.

Neither my husband nor the children know I'm seeing Dr Felsenberg and it's much better that way. At the time of our weekly session, I'm officially attending a yoga class, which only exists on the kitchen calendar.

So I talk to myself to reassure, console and encourage myself. I speak familiarly, since the two parts of me have known each other for a long time. I'm well aware that this may seem ridiculous. Or worrying. But the fact is that the part of me that talks to the other always appears confident and reassuring. She sees the best in everything, always looks on the bright side and mostly gets the last word. She's not the sort to panic.

And in the evening when I go to bed it's not unusual for her to congratulate me.

The two parts of me have always existed. The concerned parties, so to speak, but until recently they didn't communicate with each other, at least not through the medium of my voice. That's much more recent.

Dr Felsenberg also asked me if an event or an episode had created or triggered this voice. As I was thinking in silence, he rephrased the question.

He wanted to know if I'd ever talked to myself when I was a girl or a student, for example. Or when I was first married. Or when I stopped work. I was certain I hadn't.

'It's not a problem in itself, you know. Lots of people talk to themselves,' Dr Felsenberg said. 'But it is a problem for you, because you've brought it up.' He wanted me to think about it. He decided we would reflect together on the function of these exchanges between me and myself.

———

It took a few sessions for me to realise (and acknowledge) that the voice appeared shortly before the discovery I made on my husband's computer. And a few more sessions to talk explicitly about this discovery in Dr Felsenberg's office.

What I saw that day, and what I saw on the days that followed, when I started to look, I can only express indirectly, through circumlocutions. I'm unable to set it down in black and white.

Because the words are vile and stained with dread.

Last night when I got home I found Mathis and his friend there. Normally at that time they should have been in school. My son claimed the music teacher was absent and I could tell at once that he was lying.

They looked odd. Both of them. Mathis doesn't like me going into his room, so I stayed at the door, waiting, trying to work out what was wrong. They were sitting on the floor. It was tidy. They hadn't got any games or books out. I wondered what they were up to. Théo was looking down. He was staring at a point on the carpet as though he was observing a colony of microscopic insects that only he could see.

I have a problem with that boy. To be honest, I don't like him. I know it's horrible to think that. He's just a twelve-year-old boy, pretty well brought up on the whole, but there's just something about him that bothers me. I've been careful not to share this with Mathis, who idolises him as though he has supernatural powers, but I don't get on with him. I really don't understand what he sees in him. When he was in primary school, Mathis had a friend I really liked. They got on brilliantly and never fought. But that kid moved away at the end of primary school.

Last year when Mathis started secondary, he met Théo and from then on nothing else mattered. He became attached to him immediately and exclusively and defends him tooth and nail if I ever express the tiniest reservation or ask anything about him.

I asked them if they'd had tea and my son said they weren't hungry. I let them be.

Nonetheless I can't help feeling that Théo is dragging Mathis down a slippery slope, that he's having a bad influence on him. He's tougher than our son, less emotional. That's probably why Mathis thinks so much of him. The other day after dinner I tried to talk to my husband about it. Since I discovered how William really spends his evenings, apart from the largely prosaic exchanges that allow us to maintain a life together, I have not been tempted to communicate with him. To tell the truth, I'd just spent weeks observing his little tricks and lies from a distance.

After dinner he retired to his study as usual.

I knocked on the door. I was tempted to go in without waiting for his response; it was an unexpected opportunity to surprise him in the act. It was several seconds before he permitted me to enter. The computer screen was blank. He'd taken off his jacket and had some papers spread out in front of him. I sat down in the armchair and began talking about Mathis and the negative influence I felt his friend was having. I explained why I had the feeling that this relationship was disturbing our son and gave a few random examples. William seemed to be listening carefully and was not showing impatience. As I reached the end of my little speech, this phrase came into my mind: *here you are, confronting the devil in his lair.* It was ridiculous and completely over the top. If William had heard me he would probably once again have mocked my affected figures of speech. But from that moment I have not been able to shake off that phrase and its powerful reverberation. William wanted hard facts. Signs of regression, a graph showing decline, quantifiable evidence. What evidence could I put on record? Mathis's school results were very respectable. He didn't see what the problem was. I was imagining things. The fact is, William always thinks I'm imagining things. About everything. It has become an effective way to gently bring any conversation to an end. 'You're imagining things.'

The truth is, most of what I tell my husband holds very little interest for him. It's one of the reasons I tell him almost nothing. It hasn't always been like this. When we first met, we spent entire nights talking. I learned almost everything from William. Words, gestures, the way I stand, laugh, behave. He held the codes and the keys.

I don't know when we stopped talking. A long time ago, for sure. But the most worrying part is that I didn't realise.

This morning, Mathis got up before me. When I went into the kitchen he was making his breakfast.

I sat down and watched him for a few minutes: the nonchalance with just a hint of cockiness in the way he picked things up, let the cupboards close automatically, the embarrassment on his face whenever I speak to him or ask a question. I understood then that he was on the threshold, right on the threshold. It's already stirring and incubating in him like a virus, at work in every cell of his body even if nothing is perceptible to the naked eye. Mathis isn't an adolescent yet, at least not visibly so. But it's a just matter of weeks, perhaps days.

My little boy is going to be transformed before our eyes just as his sister was, and nothing will be able to stop it.

MATHIS

On his first day at secondary school he chose the middle row. And then his seat: in the middle of the middle row. Not too far from the board and not too near it. Neither the front nor the back. Where he expected to attract least attention. From the list pinned up in the playground he'd realised that he wouldn't know any of the other pupils. Everyone from his primary school had been split up between other classes.

By the time the door closed, no one had sat down beside him. He didn't dare look at the others, sitting in pairs, elbow to elbow, busy whispering. All round the class the murmuring had begun, a low, drifting hum that the teacher, for now, was managing to control. He was excluded from their secrets. He had never felt so alone. So vulnerable. The girls in front had already turned round twice to size him up.

Ten minutes later someone knocked at the door. The education advisor came in with a pupil Mathis had never seen before. Théo Lubin had got lost in the corridors and been unable to find his class. A derisive whistle ran through the rows. The teacher pointed to the empty seat beside Mathis. Théo sat down. Mathis pushed aside his own things, though they weren't in the way, as a way of greeting the latecomer, of signalling to him that he was welcome. He tried to catch his eye to smile at him, but Théo kept his head down. He took out his pencil case and exercise book and without looking up muttered, 'Thanks.'

In the next lesson they sat together again.

On the days that followed they looked for the gym together, the head of year's office, the canteen and room numbers that defied all logic. They mastered this new space, which then seemed endless and which they now know like the backs of their hands.

They didn't need to talk to know they'd get on. They only had to look at each other to see something silently shared – social, affective, emotional – abstract, fleeting signs of mutual recognition which they wouldn't have been able to name. They've been together ever since.

Mathis knows how much Théo's silence impresses others. Girls as well as boys. Théo doesn't say much, but he's not the sort to be pushed around. He's feared. Respected. He's never had to fight, or even threaten to. But there's something menacing within him that dissuades attack and comments. When he's beside him, Mathis is protected, not at risk.

———

On the first day of school this year, when Mathis saw on the noticeboard that they were in the same class again, he felt an intense sense of relief. If asked, he wouldn't have been able to say whether he felt relief for himself or for Théo. Today, a few months later, it seems to him as though his friend has grown even more sombre. He often has the feeling that Théo is playing a role, that he's pretending. He's there beside him, going from class to class, waiting patiently in the canteen queue, tidying his things, his locker, his tray, but in reality he's standing outside it all. And sometimes when they say goodbye at Monoprix, when he lets Théo go off towards the metro, a confused fear spreads in his chest that stops him breathing.

Mathis is stealing money from his mother. She doesn't suspect. She leaves her bag lying around, doesn't check her change. He goes for coins, never notes. And he takes them carefully: one or two at a time, never more. That's enough for small bottles: €5 for La Martiniquaise rum, €6 for Poliakov vodka. They go to the little grocer's at the end of the street. He's more expensive than elsewhere, but he never asks questions. For big bottles, the best bet is to go through Hugo's brother Baptiste, who's in his second-last year at the high school nearby. He's still underage but looks older than he is. He can go to the supermarket and not get asked for his identity card.

He asks them for 'a small percentage'. On good days, he'll do a discount.

Mathis hides the coins in an ebony box his sister gave him. He thought it looked like a girl's thing because the inside was lined with floral fabric, but the box has the advantage of locking and now it hides his treasure.

Tomorrow after lunch they have a study period. If there's no one in the corridor, they'll slip into their hiding place to drink the rum they bought yesterday. Théo said that it makes your head *explode*, even more than vodka. He pointed an imaginary pistol at his temple, two fingers together, and pretended to fire.

THÉO

He's left the big pullover he got for Christmas at his father's, the one his mother asked him not to take there. She didn't realise at once, but today, now that it's got colder, she's surprised he isn't wearing it. She's horribly angry, that's obvious. She's struggling to mask the signs of irritation that Théo knows well. She says several times: 'We're not likely to see that again.' The pullover is in danger, absorbed into the depths of the void. She's alluding to the enemy territory that she will not name. A place governed by unknown laws, where clothes can take weeks to be washed and where objects get lost and never reappear.

Théo promises he'll bring it next time. No, he won't forget.

She's finding it hard to let it go, he can see.

When he was younger, up until the end of primary school, she packed his bag for him before he went to his father's. She chose his least nice, most worn clothes on the grounds that they took ages to come back and sometimes never came back at all. On Friday evening she took him *there* on the metro and left him outside the building. At the start, when Théo was too young to take the lift on his own, his father would come down and be watching from the other side of the glass doors. Like a hostage exchanged for some unknown commodity, Théo would go down the hall and cross the neutral zone, scarcely daring to press the light switch. A week later, at the same time on Friday, on a different street, his father would switch off his engine and wait in the car for Théo to go into the building and start the whole thing again. In another stairwell, his mother would hug him tight. Between kisses, she'd stroke his face and hair, looking him over with relief, as though he had returned miraculously alive from some unfathomable disaster.

He remembers one day a long time ago – he must have been seven or eight – when his mother was checking the contents of his bag after he came back from his father's, she didn't find the trousers she'd bought him a few weeks earlier. She began taking all the clothes out one by one, as though it were a matter of life and death, tossing them angrily in the air. And then, having confirmed that the garment was missing, she began to cry. Théo watched her, stunned. His mother was kneeling in front of a sports bag, her body wracked with sobs. He could see her pain, it struck him in jolts, but there was something that escaped him: why was it so serious?

His mother had begun complaining that his father couldn't give a shit about getting his things together (every time she said something bad about his father, this wrenching feeling of discomfort agitated his stomach and the sharp sound made his ears buzz) and he had to admit that he'd packed his bag himself. He'd done his best to collect up his clothes, but he hadn't found his trousers, which were probably in the wash. And then suddenly his mother had shouted, 'Doesn't that slut know how to turn a washing machine on?'

When his parents divorced, his father moved in to a new apartment, where he still lives. He put up an extra partition at the back of the living room so that Théo could have a room of his own. In the months after the separation, his father was seeing another woman whom his mother called 'the bitch' or 'the slut'. The bitch came to his father's some evenings but never slept over. She worked in the same company as him. They must have got to know each other in the lift or the canteen; that was how Théo imagined them meeting, a scene he tried to reconstruct several times, despite his difficulty conceiving the setting. He found it impossible to imagine what 'the office', the place his father went each day on the other side of the ring road, looked like.

He remembers a spring day at the botanical gardens with his father and this woman. He must have been six or seven. He'd been on the trampoline and the go-carts, had a go at the coconut shy. Later in the afternoon, all three of them got lost in the maze of mirrors, then they climbed into a boat and, for what seemed like a deliciously long time to him, they allowed themselves to be carried along by the current of the enchanted river. Later they had candyfloss. The bitch was nice. It was thanks to her that they'd discovered this marvellous world, protected by gates and fences, a world where children were kings. This woman must have had some connection to this place, she knew every corner. She was the one who had guided them along its paths and handed out the tickets, and his father looked at her with such devotion that Théo came to the conclusion that the whole garden must belong to her.

But the next day when he went back to his mother, he had stomach ache. He felt sad. Guilty. He'd had fun with this woman, accepted her gifts.

Something sweet and sticky still clung to his hands.

At the start, when he got back from his father's, his mother would ask him questions. While pretending not to get involved, as though he couldn't spot her ploy, she would fish for information by means of digressions and circumlocutions that he saw through immediately.

To say as little as possible, Théo pretended not to understand the questions, or else he replied evasively.

Back then, his mother would suddenly begin crying without warning, because she couldn't open a jam jar or find something that had disappeared or because the television had stopped working or because she was tired. Sometimes it was like an electric shock, sometimes a cut or a punch, but his body always connected with her pain and absorbed its share.

At the start, every time he came back from his father's, she asked him, 'Did you have fun? You didn't cry? Did you think about Mummy?' He couldn't have explained why, but he instantly felt this was a trap. He never knew whether he was supposed to reassure his mother by telling her it had all gone well or claim that he'd been bored and had missed her. One day, when Théo had probably struck her as too happy after his week *on the other side*, his mother's face took on a horribly sad expression. She became silent and he was afraid she'd start crying again. But after a few minutes, she said in a small voice, 'All that matters is that you're happy. If you don't need me, I'll go, you know. Go travelling, maybe. Have a rest.'

Théo learned very quickly to play the role expected of him. To offer words sparingly, expressionlessly, eyes lowered. Not to expose himself. On both sides of the frontier, silence was clearly the best policy, the least dangerous.

———

After a time, he couldn't say when, *the bitch* disappeared. According to what he managed to glean at the time from scraps of phone conversations caught on one side or the other, the woman had children, who couldn't have appreciated her having fun at the botanical gardens without them, and a husband she didn't want to leave.

Gradually, his mother stopped crying. She sold the furniture and bought newer, nicer furniture, then she repainted the apartment. Théo chose the colours for his room and the kitchen.

She stopped questioning him when he came back from a week with his father. She no longer asked what he'd done or with whom. If he'd had fun. In fact, she started avoiding the subject. She didn't want to know anything any more.

Today, the time he spends away from her has ceased to exist. One evening she explained to Théo that she had drawn a line under *all that* and no longer wanted to hear it mentioned.

His father does not exist. She has stopped uttering his name.

HÉLÈNE

I wanted to bring up Théo Lubin's case at the next student welfare meeting. Frédéric convinced me to wait a bit longer. He feels I don't have enough evidence. Also, bringing up a case always leaves traces, which might harm Théo or his family down the line, and that's not something that should be treated lightly.

Did I appear to be treating it lightly? I wake up every night, my breathing constricted by anxiety, and it often takes me hours to get back to sleep. I no longer want to go out with my friends or to the cinema. I refuse to have fun. Anyway, there is no 'case'. I have no documents to add to the file and I'd have to go against the advice of the nurse, who didn't think it was a good idea to call in the parents, though so far she hasn't had any reply to the letter she sent home to the mother.

I agreed to wait a bit. Frédéric promised he'd pay particular attention to Théo, though he only has his class for one hour a week.

Yesterday afternoon, when I saw Théo come into class just after Mathis, my heart gave a lurch. I was sorry I'd given in. He immediately struck me as odd, unsteady. He was walking carefully, as though at every step the ground might give way beneath him. What a sight the poor kid was, leaning on the tables to get to his. That really got to me. He looked like a drunk. I thought he'd injured his leg or his back, he was having such difficulty moving forward. Then he collapsed into his chair, looking relieved to have made it that far. His eyes were fixed on the floor, avoiding mine.

By the time all the students had sat down and the hubbub subsided, he still hadn't moved. I asked him why he hadn't taken his exercise book out. Without looking up at me, in a thin voice, he replied that he'd forgotten it.

I felt panic flood through me. Images that I couldn't block out assailed me. I couldn't calm my mind or get my breath back. I couldn't stop looking at him, trying to understand what was going on.

Then I saw the injuries on his body. I saw them as clearly as if his clothes were ripped in exactly the right places to reveal the bruises and the blood. I was gasping for air. I looked at the other students. I watched their faces for the moment when they would realise. I hoped that one of them, just one of them, could see what I saw. But they were all motionless, waiting for the sentence I was going to pronounce or for the lesson to begin. I repeated these words in my head several times: *I'm the only one who can see his injuries. I'm the only one who can see he's bleeding.* I closed my eyes and tried to reason with myself, to calm my breathing, to recall the words of the nurse who had examined him and her firm, reassuring tone: 'There was nothing. No mark, no trace, no scar.'

There was nothing.

Except: I've been hit, so with me that won't wash.

Hugo in the front row asked me gently, 'Miss, are you feeling ill?'

The images were fighting back.

I took a deep breath and asked the students to take out a piece of paper, then I read out the test questions without going to the trouble of writing them on the board.

'What is the function of the foods we consume each day?'

'List the food groups that you know.'

'What unit of measurement is used to calculate the energy foods provide?'

One of the girls in the front row (Rose Jacquin probably, who never misses a chance to pipe up) interrupted me: 'Miss, you're going too quick!'

I had never given them a surprise test before and a ripple of dissent ran through the room. Théo still had his head down, his hands shielding his eyes like a visor so that I could no longer see them. I asked if he wanted to go to the nurse and he said no.

The students, who'd been incredulous at first, eventually settled and got down to work. On the grounds of preventing any chatting, I was now able to observe him. His body was inclined slightly forward, his pen raised. He had put his free hand on his paper as though for support. It was as if he couldn't focus his attention on his work; his eyes were looking for some anchor point but couldn't find one.

After a few minutes I walked through the rows. As I passed him, I saw he hadn't written anything. He had a film of sweat on his forehead. I had an urge to stroke his hair. I had an urge to sit down beside him and give him a hug.

I walked past his table several times, but he never raised his head to look at me. I no longer figured in his field of vision.

Maybe he was annoyed with me because of the nurse. He was indicating to me that I had betrayed him, that I no longer deserved his trust.

I returned to my place at the desk. In silence I managed to calm down and pretend I was marking exercise books.

When the bell rang, I asked Rose to collect the tests. As she came to pick up Théo's and Mathis's, she stopped.

She gave a high laugh, though I couldn't tell if it was one of surprise or complicity.

I watched the students file out. Théo was walking with a little more confidence, but something was wrong, I was sure of it. Something I didn't understand.

When the room was empty, I sorted through the tests until I found his. In the margin he'd simply written his first name. He hadn't copied down the questions or attempted to answer them.

He had, however, tried to draw one of the diagrams illustrating the digestive system that I had given out in class a few days before. In a style that was simple but precise he had drawn the outline of the human body from the head to the waist. Within this shape he had represented the mouth, oesophagus, stomach, and the intestine coiled up on itself like a snake. At the bottom of the stomach he had drawn something that at first I took for a vegetable or flower. The drawing was unclear and I had to peer at his paper and then hold it away from me to work out that it was in fact a skull.

CÉCILE

Mathis came home from school drunk yesterday.

I saw the gleam in his eyes, the slight lack of co-ordination in his movements. I asked him to come and breathe on me so that I could smell his breath.

There wasn't a shadow of doubt.

He hadn't been drinking beer or cider. No, he'd been drinking spirits.

I'm the daughter of an alcoholic. That's how I began the session with Dr Felsenberg the next day. That was my lead-in. Even before I sat down. So that things were quite clear. My father drank every day from the moment he got home from work until late into the night. He'd repeat the same phrases until he was intoxicated, sitting in front of a bottle of table wine, preferably red. He would rail against the whole world: drivers, TV presenters, singers, neighbours, politicians, chemists, department heads, employees, attendants, delegates, to name but a few. He was never aggressive to us or our mother. That's how I saw him throughout my childhood and adolescence, sitting in front of a screen that he was barely watching, endlessly repeating the perpetual monologue that we no longer listened to. You could say he was part of the furniture. I think I always felt an indulgent affection for him, though it was tinged with shame. I never invited school friends home. He was a burnt-out man, whose sensibility was so awkward and ill-adapted to his environment that all he could do was drown it in alcohol. I never heard my mother complain. She took charge of everything: not just things related to domestic life, but also forms, official things, medical stuff, school, tax. People called her a saint. I didn't understand why, because she didn't believe in any god. But she put up with this man who had long preferred alcohol to any other form of consolation. When he lost his job, I thought he'd sink like a stone. But the programme stayed the same; the only difference was he started earlier. He remained on the surface, making no waves, with just his head above water. He rarely moved. Just enough to survive. He would sit in the same place and stick to the same rhythm (between three and five glasses an hour) and check the lights were out before going up to bed. He was allowing himself to die without making a fuss. My mother never passed comment or made the slightest protest. My elder brother did night security at an electronics warehouse for a few years. After he broke up with his girlfriend, he spent his days in his room listening to records. I looked at the colour of his skin and wondered how long he could live without seeing daylight.

One evening the television news had shown a report about an oil slick caused by a tanker accident. We were at the table. I looked at those birds caught in the sticky oil and I immediately thought of us, all of us. Those pictures represented us better than any family photo. They were us. They were our black, oily bodies, deprived of movement, numb and poisoned.

The next day all four of us set off in the car to a cousin's wedding. My brother was driving. It hadn't stopped raining all morning. The rain made a metallic sound as it bounced off the windscreen. The sky was low and seemed to be waiting to close on us like a jaw when we reached the horizon. Long streams of raindrops quivered on the side windows, held there by the wind. The noise of the windscreen wipers was audible inside the car, a wet sloshing sound, relentless, a hypnotising refrain that encouraged drowsiness. My father was sitting beside my brother in the front. He was looking ahead of him, without really looking at anything. Beside me, my mother was holding her bag on her knees, as though an unexpected signal might at any moment require her to get out of the car. I could also see that she was keeping an eye on the speedometer. Because Thierry was driving fast, very fast. Even though you couldn't see more than a few metres ahead. I'd already asked him once to slow down. He pretended not to hear. A few minutes later, when we were going even faster, I asked him more sharply. My brother muttered something to suggest he had the situation under control and then got on the tail of the car in front to force it to allow us to overtake it. My father was staring at a point in front of him, with that look of having given up that I had known for ever. My mother was hunched over her bag. But I could see the spray thrown back by the cars we were overtaking one after another, then their tail lights began to dance before my eyes, and then all the lights started to blur together.

Dead silence had filled the car.

Then I thought of the expression *breakneck speed*. The deadly atmosphere that suddenly overwhelmed me was not confined to the car, it was how we had been living for years. I began to scream.

'Stop! Stop now! I want to get out of the car!'

Stunned, my brother slowed down.

'I want to get out of this car! Stop! Let me out! I want to get out! I want to get out!'

I was shrieking like I was crazy.

Thierry stopped at the next lay-by a few hundred metres further on. He pulled up abruptly and I kept repeating the same phrase, 'I want to get out, I want to get out, do you understand? I want to get out.' But actually what I was shouting was, 'I want to live,' as they knew full well.

I got out of the car. Without saying anything, my father opened his door, walked round and opened

Thierry's door. My brother quickly moved over to give him the driving seat. My father nodded to me to get back in the car and I shook my head. My whole body was shaking.

He hesitated for a second, then started the engine.

When I think back to that moment, to the final glance he shot me before he rejoined the traffic, I know my father understood that day that I was going to leave them. That I was going to launch myself into different worlds, different ways of being, and that one day we would probably no longer speak the same language.

I watched our car drive away. I was at the side of a main road. In the distance I could see the outline of a town or a village. I began walking. After a few minutes a woman stopped and offered me a lift.

I come from a family where people say 'my cousin could of' and 'my sister should of'. And we say 'Auntie Nadine' or 'Nunky Jacques'. 'Look what I done.' 'We're going up the town.' We eat our *tea* every evening at the set time in front of the television news. Just to make things quite clear.

When I met William, I discovered a universe with customs and taboos I knew nothing about. He would gently pick me up when I made mistakes. Later he congratulated me on my progress. I read dozens of books and learned quickly. He was proud of me. When

Sonia was born, or rather when she started saying her first words, he told me that it was out of the question that she should call my mother 'Nana' or my brother 'Nunky Thierry'. Rules were laid down. We've raised our children to speak *his* language. They say 'Grandmother' and 'Grandfather'. They go to Paris, not 'up the town'. They have dinner in the evening, never tea.

This is what I said, as chaotically as this and in a continuous stream (to be honest, like someone who hadn't opened their mouth for several years), to explain to Dr Felsenberg the strength of my reaction when I discovered Mathis had been drinking.

Of course, I immediately thought that it came from me, that it was my fault. He's not yet thirteen and he's drinking alcohol. Isn't that proof that something is dormant in him, just waiting to burst out, roaring? Something that of course comes from me, from 'my side'? Because I was quite certain that if I spoke to William about it he'd ask, 'Who does he get that from?'

But I had no desire to talk to William about it.

It was well worth expending so much time and energy blending into the background and eliminating everything in me that offended the ears of my husband and his family, trying to pass on elegant turns of phrase and genteel manners to my children.

It was well worth learning to say 'Mathis could have' and 'Sonia should have', just to end up here.

HERO

THÉO

When he got out of school, he needed air, needed to stretch his legs. He couldn't go straight home. That was too risky.

After twenty minutes the feeling of drunkenness had worn off. His breath made a little vapour cloud in the cold air. The alcohol was evaporating.

Just before seven, he opened the apartment door and checked the coast was clear. For a few months, his mother had been doing a gym class at the end of the day on Friday. This spared them both the tense moment of parting, with all the things that couldn't be said and unspoken recommendations. Generally he sends her a message a bit later to let her know he's arrived safely. She makes do with an 'OK' in reply.

Then the connection is broken for a week. Over and out.

He's looked everywhere for his coat but hasn't found it. He looked in the dirty washing and checked it wasn't drying.

In a few minutes Théo has gathered together the rest of his things for the week. He's turned off all the lights and locked the door behind him.

He takes the overhead metro to the place d'Italie.

He gets to his father's building.

He would like to have hung on to a vague feeling of drunkenness in some distant corner of his brain so that he could now regain access to it. He searches within himself for a trace of intoxication. He'd like to recover alcohol's influence over his movements – a slowness, a drowsiness, however tiny – but it's all gone. He's lost his carapace. He's burned it all up in the winter air. He's become the child he hates again, who feels fear in his stomach as he presses the lift button. The fear emerges from a numb sleep whose golden taste has gone. It spreads through his whole body and increases his heart rate.

When Théo rings the bell, it takes his father several minutes to open the door. The last time he waited for almost half an hour. He could hear him inside, or at least sense his presence, a breathing or a scraping, but his father wasn't ready to open the door, to welcome him, as though the increasing amount of time he needed to come to the door would enable him to become human again. That's what he reckons today as he waits on the doormat, that his father needs all this time to be able to face him. He has the key for downstairs but not the one for this lock, which his father turns when he wants to be sure he won't be disturbed. So Théo eventually sits on the top step and waits. And every eighty seconds he gets up to press the timer switch.

When his father appears at last, even if Théo has spent all day preparing himself for this image, even if he has mentally pictured it dozens of times to get himself used to it, even if he has known for several months that he'll find him in this state, he finds it hard to conceal the movement of recoil that his body makes in spite of himself. Recoil and revulsion, because every time it's worse than the last, as though it's possible to keep sinking deeper into self-neglect. In a fraction of a second, Théo registers everything: the pyjamas, the egg or urine stain around the crotch, the beard, the smell, the bare feet in flip-flops, the nails that are too long, the dilated pupils trying to adjust to the presence of another human being.

And then his father smiles at him, with a sort of sad-looking grimace.

His father used to pull him towards him and give him a hug, but he no longer dares. He smells bad and he knows it.

Next he goes back to bed or sits at his desk in front of the computer. He makes a superhuman effort to ask some questions. Théo could describe every little detail of the slow progress of this effort, its cogs and gears, whose unbearable rusty creaking he thinks he can almost hear. The time his father takes to think up his questions and then ask them. In a sort of failed ritual, he asks for news about school, the handball team (which Théo quit almost a year ago), but he's incapable of concentrating on his answers. Théo always ends up getting irritated because his father asks him the same question twice or because he only pretends to listen. Sometimes he tries to confuse him, to catch him out not paying attention; he suddenly asks him to repeat what he just said and then lets him get tangled up in some words, which his brain has superficially retained in a vain attempt to put them together again. Actually, his father doesn't do too badly. Then Théo can't stop himself smiling at him; he says, 'It's OK, don't worry, I'll tell you another time.'

Later, he'll sort through the leftovers in the refrigerator, throwing out what's rotten or mouldy, checking the use-by dates. He'll strip his father's bed and open the windows to air the rooms. If there's any washing powder left, he'll put the machine on. He'll run the dishwasher. Or he'll let the plates soak because of the food, which is sometimes so dry it seems encrusted on.

Then he'll go back downstairs with his father's bank card and go to the cash machine. First he'll try to get

€50. If the machine refuses, he'll start again and try for €20. It doesn't give out tens.

He'll go to the supermarket.

When he gets back, he'll try to convince his father to get up, have a wash and get dressed. He'll raise the electric blind and go and talk to him in his room. He'll try to drag him outside, at least for a bit of a walk. He'll call to him from the living room several times to come and watch a film or a television programme together.

Or maybe he won't do any of that.

This time he may no longer have the strength. Perhaps he'll just let things go, without trying to repair them, to put them in order. Perhaps he'll simply sit in the dark, letting his legs swing between the legs of the chair, because he no longer knows what to say or do, because he knows all this is too much for him, that he isn't strong enough.

He doesn't remember how long it's been since his father stopped working. Two years? Three? He knows that one evening he promised to keep quiet about it. Because if his mother finds out that his father is no longer working, she'll go to court to seek sole custody. That's what his father said.

He promised not to mention it, which is why he didn't say anything to his grandmother, or to his father's sister, who sometimes called.

———

Before, his father used to work too much. He got back late from the office, spent the evening in front of the computer, stayed up late. One day he got *suspended* by his company. Théo has never forgotten that word: *suspended*. He immediately imagined his father hoisted off the ground, kept there helpless, at the whim of some line manager as a sign of victory and domination. What it really meant was that his father was no longer allowed to return to work, have access to his files or his computer. Had he done something wrong? Made a serious mistake? Théo had been too young for his father to explain to him what happened, but he had retained this image of the terrible humiliation that had destroyed him.

His father had spent a few months looking for a job. He'd taken a course to broaden his skills, had gone back to English classes. He'd gone to meetings, had interviews.

And then gradually the contacts his father maintained with the outside world became fewer and fewer. And then everything that sustained his connection with others, everything that was cause for hope he would one day start a new job, everything that made him leave the apartment, broke. Théo didn't realise at once, because this rupture happened without drama or fireworks – unlike the rupture between his parents, which had made them tear each other to pieces for months in a relentless struggle, with lawyers as their intermediaries and him as the witness condemned to silence. At first his father had started hanging around home a bit more, in the morning or the afternoon. He loved spending time with him. They'd go for a drive; his father would drive with one hand, relaxed, and say, 'This is good, isn't it, just us two?' He was planning to take him to London or Berlin when he had topped up the coffers. And then he stopped driving because there was no fuel in the car. And then he stopped leaving the flat. And then he sold the car. And then he limited the time he spent away from his bed or the living-room sofa as much as possible. Now he rents his parking space to a neighbour for €100 a month and this money represents a significant proportion of his income.

Théo doesn't know how long it's been since they went on an outing, played cards or Ludo, or how long it is since his father made dinner, turned on the oven, how long since he raised the blinds for himself, put on a wash, emptied the bin.

Nor does he know how long it's been since his grandmother, grandfather, uncle and aunt visited, how long his father has been on medication, has spent all day dozing, hardly ever washing, how long there have been weeks when they have to feed themselves on €20.

MATHIS

He's not allowed to see his friends at the weekend because his mother noticed he'd been drinking. She conducted her interrogation methodically. Since they're not allowed out during their study periods, she wanted to know what ruse he'd used to manage to drink inside the school. Had he finished an hour early? Had he left without permission? Within a few minutes, Mathis had invented a whole story: a girl in his class had brought in a little bottle of rum to make a cake and they'd shared what was left of that. It tasted a bit sugary and spicy; they didn't realise how much they'd had. He had the sort of mother who would believe they still baked cakes in school. She wanted to know if Théo was with them (she's convinced that Théo is behind everything). With a confidence that surprised even him, he said no. Théo had been absent.

In the end she let it drop. This time she wouldn't say anything to his father. But she warned him: if it happened again, if she found out that he'd drunk alcohol in or out of school, she wouldn't hesitate to tell him.

He wasn't allowed to play on his games console either. He wasn't allowed to contact anyone at all because she'd confiscated his mobile. In any case, when Théo is at his dad's, they never meet up.

On Saturday afternoon Mathis went with her to buy new trainers because his old ones were starting to pinch. When they left the shop, they went to see his big sister, who lives with a friend near Montparnasse Cemetery, and drop off the shopping his mother said she'd get her. They had tea with Sonia, then they walked home. On the way they looked at the film posters and discussed which ones they'd like to see.

All afternoon, he noticed his mother had that vague sadness that he hates because he can't shake off the feeling that he's responsible for it. There's a certain tone in her voice that he alone seems to catch and a way she has of looking at him as though he's become an adult overnight and is preparing to depart for the other end of the earth. Or as though he's committed some mistake that he's completely unaware of.

On Monday morning he met Théo outside school. His friend had done some research over the weekend; he had plans he was keen to tell Mathis about.

When Mr Châle collected the money that the parents were supposed to send for the evening at the Opéra

Garnier, Théo said that his mother didn't want him to go because of the terrorist attacks. Mr Châle hesitated for a moment and was about to ask some more questions, but then thought better of it.

Mathis knows this isn't true. It's not because of his mother. Théo isn't going because he doesn't have the money. And it's not the first time.

HÉLÈNE

I realised that we didn't have the father's address, which is normally on the forms the students fill in at the start of the year. We didn't even have his phone number to contact him in case of an emergency. I decided to ask to see the mother without any particular motive. I didn't go through Théo or the school's website. I sent a brief note in the mail with my telephone number, asking her to contact me as soon as possible. She rang me the same day, her voice betraying her worry. Théo hadn't given her the nurse's message, that's why she hadn't replied. I don't know why, but I really didn't warm to her right from the start. She said that Théo was at his father's till Friday and she could come in one evening that suited me after 6 p.m. I arranged to see her the next day.

In the distance I saw a fragile figure walking quickly across the playground. She was in a belted beige raincoat.

She wasn't wearing a scarf or jewellery. The colour of her clothes, the way she moved and held her bag all indicated how much she wanted to live up to expectations, to strike the right note. I went out to meet her and we went upstairs to the science lab. She wasn't at all like the woman I had imagined.

I began talking about Théo. I said I thought he looked tired, exhausted. That he had increasing difficulty following the lesson. He'd been to the nurse several times and hadn't answered any of the questions in the last test. At first she appeared not to understand; her son's results were good, she didn't see what the problem was.

I said, 'The problem is that there's something the matter with your son. I am not questioning his ability. I'm talking about him, about his increasing difficulty with concentrating.'

She looked at me for several seconds. I'm certain she was trying to gauge my power to cause trouble; she was calculating the risk of telling me to get lost there and then: *What business is it of yours?*

She adopted a soft but firm tone that must make quite an impression in a professional situation.

'My son is absolutely fine. He's an adolescent who has trouble getting to sleep and who probably spends too much time staring at a screen like all young people of his age.'

I'm not the sort to let things drop that easily.

'He's a bit young at twelve.'

'He'll be thirteen in a few days.'

'Do you have any idea what kind of life he leads when he's at his father's? Does he have a regular timetable?'

She took a breath before replying.

'My husband left me six years ago and we no longer have any contact.'

'Even about Théo?'

'No. He's not a child. We have joint custody.'

'Does that work for him?'

'My ex-husband insisted on it to reduce his maintenance payments. Which he doesn't pay anyway.'

I could feel a blind rage against this woman building in me, something dark and fierce flooding into me, which I couldn't contain. I sensed the steeliness beneath her fragile appearance; I wanted to see her retreat into her protection zone, to feel her fold.

'You refuse to let Théo go on school trips. That's a pity, because trips are an important time for class bonding.'

Her surprise was not the sort that can easily be faked.

'You mean he doesn't take part in trips?'

'No, not a single one.'

I wanted to go further. I wanted to throw her off balance.

'If it's a question of money, you could ask for help from the office ...'

She raised her voice to interrupt. 'It's not about money, Ms Destrée. But when he's at his father's, his father is the one who ought to pay.'

I let the words hang for a few moments.

'The Head is also surprised that you never come to parents' evenings.'

'I don't come because I can't risk bumping into my ex-husband … I … I'd find that hard to bear.'

'We have never seen your ex-husband either, and I'm not sure that he has been informed about these evenings. Since you haven't seen fit to give us his details.'

She paused. She was trying to understand.

'It was Théo who filled in the forms. At the start of the year when he got me to sign them, I noticed he hadn't put down his father's address, you're right, but he told me he'd add it later.'

I could sense she was faltering. A doubt had fractured her defence system.

I wanted to hurt her. Hurtful words and sarcastic remarks came to my mind that I had difficulty holding back. I hadn't felt that for years.

This woman wasn't protecting her child and that made me furious.

'Was your ex-husband violent?'

'No, not at all. Why are you asking that?'

I had crossed a red line. The red line was far behind me.

'You know, by the time children are found in a pit or at the end of a rope, it's too late.'

She looked at me as though I were possessed. She looked around for a witness or some support. But we were alone in the science lab, white and tiled, surrounded by lab benches and microscopes, a smell of disinfectant in the air reminiscent of a hospital. At the back of the class, a tap was dripping as regularly as a metronome.

Then, without warning, she covered her face with her hands and began to cry. Taken aback, I clumsily attempted to backpedal.

'Listen, a few of us have noticed something wrong with Théo. He's withdrawn. There's a risk he'll switch off.'

She kept crying while hunting for something in her bag. She kept saying, 'I don't understand.' There was no arrogance left in her, no posturing. I noticed traces of foundation on her neck that she hadn't blended in properly and blotches that her make-up didn't conceal. The collar of her blouse was a little frayed and her hands looked very worn for her age. She was a woman whom life had treated harshly. A woman whose dream had been crushed and who was trying to put a brave face on it.

I suddenly felt ashamed of having made her come in and subjecting her to this. With no valid reason.

I had to bring the meeting to a close, calm things down, restore some semblance of normality. I eventually handed her a Kleenex.

'I think you ought to take Théo to the doctor. Check he's OK, that he doesn't have ... deficiencies ... The extent of his tiredness worries us. That's the nurse's opinion too.'

She pulled herself together as quickly as she had fallen apart. She said she'd make an appointment the following day and told me she'd ask Théo about school trips.

We parted at the bottom of the stairs.

I watched her go off across the playground. She looked back at me one last time before she went through the gate, as though she was checking I wasn't following her.

I took my phone from my bag and called Frédéric.

He picked up after the first ring and I said, 'I've screwed up. Big time.'

THÉO

He was last to come into the gym. The students were sitting in a circle on the mats. Mrs Berthelot was standing near the door, waiting for any stragglers for her usual sports-kit check.

By 'sports kit' Mrs Berthelot meant the full thing: tracksuit top and bottoms, and real sports shoes, none of those space shoes or other flashy designs.

A few weeks ago Théo received a punishment: he had to copy out fifty times: 'I must bring my kit for PE class on Tuesday at 2 p.m.'

Today when he passed her, she gesticulated at him to stop.

'Don't you have your tracksuit?'

He explained that he was at his dad's this week and that before he left his mum's he'd looked everywhere for it but couldn't find it.

'Don't you have a tracksuit at your father's?'

He shook his head, but she'd decided not to let it drop.

'Can't your father buy you a tracksuit?'

No, his father couldn't buy him one. His father no longer qualified for benefits, no longer left home, and shuffled around like a zombie.

He could have spilled out the whole story, there and then, and he would have had the fleeting impression that he'd scored a point. But he knows she's stubborn and likes to have the last word. And anyway, she wouldn't have been able to take him seriously.

She's still complaining. She's had enough, really *e-nough*, of students who think they can do what they like and turn up in their street clothes as though this was a game of dominoes in their living room. Who do they think they are?

She's still standing in his way. The sentence eventually comes: 'Take some bottoms from the lost property box and go and change.'

This is an order, but Théo doesn't move.

'Off you go!'

She knows full well there is just one pair of tracksuit bottoms in the box, where they've been mouldering for the past ten years. What's more, they've pink and tiny.

Théo makes a final protest and then takes out the jogging bottoms and shows them to her, so that she realises. He holds them with his fingertips, hoping she'll recoil.

'Put them on and do four circuits of the gym.'

Théo mutters that the tracksuit bottoms smell.

'That will teach you not to always forget your things.'

She has no intention of giving in. It's out of the question that she'll start the lesson until he has changed and done his four laps.

Théo goes to the changing rooms and comes back a few minutes later. The pink jogging bottoms come up to his mid-calf. He's expecting to be greeted with sniggers and taunts, but no one laughs. Mathis keeps saying, 'It's not fair, Miss.' Mrs Berthelot tells him to be quiet or he will be punished too.

The class has stopped talking. The gym has never been so quiet.

Théo starts to move. Slowly, with short strides, he does the four circuits he's been told to in deathly silence.

He feels a wave of heat come to his cheeks. He can't remember ever feeling such shame.

From where they are, can the others see that the cuffs on the jogging bottoms have an embossed Barbie logo?

When he's done his four laps, there's no laughter, no comments.

He stops in front of her and she waves him towards the others sitting cross-legged on the mats.

She says, 'Good.'

Théo sits beside Mathis. When Mathis raises his head to smile at him, he sees Théo's nose is bleeding, a gush that soon stains his T-shirt, jogging bottoms and the floor mat. The girls shriek. Théo doesn't move. Mathis offers to take him to the nurse, but Mrs Berthelot picks Rose to go with him.

Amid shocked glances, Théo leaves the gym, head back with a Kleenex held to his nose.

After they've gone, Mrs Berthelot spends ten minutes cleaning up the blood.

That evening when Théo gets home, his father is sitting in the kitchen. He's got the crispbreads and jam out, poured milk into a pan and put chocolate powder into their bowls.

For a man in his state this represents considerable extra effort, the scale of which Théo appreciates. A desire to hold back from the brink of disaster, which he has observed several times in his father, a sort of last line of defence, or invisible net, which he grabs hold of and which so far has saved them from the worst.

Théo has sat down on the opposite side of the table from him. He still has the little wad of cotton wool in one nostril, a little white roll that the nurse changed just before he left school. His father seems not to have noticed.

As silence descends, Théo mentions that he spent part of the afternoon in the sickbay. A moment later, in the absence of any kind of reaction, he adds that he was punished because he didn't have any tracksuit bottoms. He describes the pink jogging bottoms and the four circuits with everyone watching.

His father's eyes start to glisten, little red spots appear on his neck and forehead and his lips tremble slightly.

Théo wants his father to stand up and bang his fist on the table. To knock things over and shout, 'I'm going to get that bitch.' To grab his parka and slam the door as he leaves the apartment.

Instead, tears start to roll down his cheeks and his hands remain on his knees.

Théo hates it when his father cries.

It's as though the noise in his head is suddenly amplified and reaches a deadly frequency. And then that makes him want to tell him he's gross and dirty and be mean to him.

Théo closes his eyes and fills his lungs with air to clear his throat – a technique he has perfected to stop himself sobbing – then hands his father a piece of kitchen roll that was lying on the table.

'It doesn't matter, Dad. Don't worry.'

HÉLÈNE

On Tuesday afternoon I passed some Year 8 girls in the corridor. They had that serious look they get when some drama's going on. They were whispering conspiratorially, but they couldn't keep the emotion they felt down to a whisper for long. Among the snippets I caught, I heard Théo's name several times. I went towards them. They fell silent as I reached them. Emma and Soline turned to Rose Jacquin, their ringleader. She'd be the one who'd reveal what they were so preoccupied with; the story would come from her if it came from anyone.

I asked where they were going. It wasn't the cleverest lead-in, but it was the best I could come up with.

They had just had PE and were supposed to be going to Frédéric's class.

I walked alongside them towards B wing. I tried to think of a way to restart the conversation, but I didn't have to; their sense of indignation was too strong to be held in check. Rose first announced to me somewhat boldly that Théo Lubin was in the sick bay.

'Something happened in PE,' she added softly.

She waited a moment, enjoying the impression she'd made, before she went on.

'He had to run by himself in front of everyone and then he had a nosebleed. A really bad one. It went everywhere, Miss.'

I didn't wait to hear the rest. I thanked her and left. I made an effort not to run, but as soon as I was out of their sight, I quickened my pace.

I knocked before going in. The curtains were drawn and the room was in semi-darkness.

I saw Théo lying on one of the beds for students. He looked asleep.

The nurse pulled the screen and indicated I should follow her into her office, a little adjoining room whose door was open. We whispered throughout our conversation. She explained that she'd had trouble staunching the bleeding and had even considered contacting the mother. No, he hadn't had a fall or made a sudden movement. Just before it started, he'd been jogging round the gymnasium. At a moderate pace, apparently, nothing too energetic. That was all he'd said. His blood pressure was low. She thought he seemed tired. She had good reason to re-examine him and so she had done so. She had looked, but there was nothing. No sign of injury. He had, though, lost weight since last time.

I asked if I could see him. She let me go over to the bed where he was lying. When he sensed my presence, he opened his eyes. His face gave nothing away.

I asked how he felt. He said he was feeling better. I asked if he wanted his parents to be contacted, and he sat up and said there was no need: his mother would get worried for no reason, the afternoon was almost over, he'd missed music, but it was the last lesson of the day. At the end of the period, he'd go home and rest.

I stayed beside him in silence. He hadn't gone under the sheets. He'd stayed on top, as though he didn't want to dirty anything, disturb anything. His T-shirt was slightly raised and I could see his skin at the top of his hip: the white skin of a child, a little boy, fragile skin, heartbreaking, so fine it seemed transparent. That was when I noticed he was wearing those horrible Barbie jogging bottoms, stained with blood.

'Are those yours?'

'No, they're from the gym. I forgot mine.'

A few minutes earlier I'd managed to catch his eye, but that was over. He pulled the sheet up over his legs.

'Was it Mrs Berthelot who told you to put on those bottoms?'

He hesitated, then nodded.

'Did she ask you to run in front of the others?'

He didn't respond.

'On your own?'

He made a silent, pained face, then closed his eyes.

I thanked the nurse and left her office.

Break was over and I was supposed to do my last lesson of the day with Year 9, who had probably already been waiting for me for several minutes in my classroom.

Without stopping to think, I headed for the gym, where Éliane Berthelot should still be.

Her students were divided into little groups around various pieces of apparatus. She was standing near the asymmetric bars, miming an exercise with her arms to explain a leg movement, which from a distance struck me as quite ridiculous.

I walked quickly up to her. I had scarcely got to her when I began shouting like a real fury, words flying from my lips in shrill bursts. I couldn't have cared less about her stunned expression and her quivering lip. I didn't give a damn about the group that soon gathered around us. Nothing else mattered, nothing could stop me (in the hours that followed it was impossible to remember what I'd said. Nothing came back to my memory apart from the sound of my anger. But since yesterday words and images have been catching up with me, as has a sense of shame). I think I came out with every insult I know, exhaustively and without omitting a single one. I'm not short of vocabulary. Éliane Berthelot eventually slapped me. Then I heard, 'They're going to fight,' and saw how keen the students were for the unprecedented spectacle we were about to offer them. The excitement was rising and some of them had already gone to the changing room to fetch their mobiles.

Suddenly reality reasserted itself. This wasn't a dream or a fantasy unfolding: I'd interrupted Éliane Berthelot's class to hurl abuse at her.

CÉCILE

A few weeks ago I went into William's study. I wasn't looking for anything in particular. Every morning when I'm alone, I go round the apartment. I pick up things that are lying around, water the plants, check that everything is OK, that everything is as it should be. I imagine that all housewives have their little daily circuit, a way of circumscribing their territory, of knowing where the limit is between inside and outside. So this particular morning I was doing my usual round.

I never spend long in William's study because of the smell of stale tobacco. Generally, I limit myself to opening the curtains and the window and come back at the end of the day to close them again. William spends most of his evenings in this study and until that day I thought he was reading the papers or preparing his files. But on this morning I'd just gone into the room when I noticed a ball of crumpled paper in the bin. I don't know why. There's often paper in William's bin and I had no reason to bend down to pick up this particular piece of paper or to open and read it. But that's what I did.

The text was in his handwriting on paper with his company's letterhead. The paragraphs had been worked on, corrected in several places, words substituted for others, and an arrow indicated that the middle paragraph was to be moved to the end. It was the draft of something quite different from the reports William writes for work. So I read it from beginning to end. In fact I stayed like that for a few minutes, stunned, reading and rereading the sentences steeped in hate and resentment, words of extraordinary virulence. I couldn't believe that William was capable of writing such things. It was impossible, unimaginable. Why had he copied out these repulsive lines? I tried to start up his computer. I was clinging on to the idea that I'd find this text in one form or another and for some obscure reason he'd copied out the writings of a madman. But his computer was password-protected. I left his study with the sheet of paper in my hand. I felt unsteady on my feet. I went to fetch my laptop from my bedroom and sat down on the sofa. I went through these motions without thinking, as though part of me already had the answers, as though this part of me was taking charge while the other rejected the evidence and struggled to remain in ignorance. I typed the first four words of William's text into the Google search bar and pressed 'Enter'. The text appeared in its entirety. It had been formatted and the corrections on the draft implemented. It was signed 'Wilmor75'. It took me a few minutes to grasp that I was looking at a blog that William had created pseudonymously, on which he regularly posted his reactions, reflections and comment on everything.

Next I entered this pseudonym in the search engine and found dozens of messages posted by Wilmor75 on news sites and discussion forums. Bitter, hateful, obscene, provocative comments, which had apparently gained him some notoriety on social networks. I spent several hours in front of the screen, stunned, shaking, clicking from page to page despite the nausea I felt. When I closed my laptop, my neck hurt. In fact, I hurt all over.

Today I'm able to describe this scene – I mean, relate how I discovered the existence of William's double. But for the first few days it was impossible for me to say anything about it at all, because there were certain words I could not utter.

It was impossible for me to imagine that my husband – the man I'd lived with for over twenty years – could use terms like 'homo', 'slut', 'ragheads', 'arsehole', 'bullshit', 'camel jockeys' and plenty more in comments whose racist, anti-Semitic, homophobic and misogynist connotations would be hard to deny. But this murky, malignant but skilful prose *was* his. It took me some time to acknowledge that it was indeed William who had been writing this blog for nearly three years, and using this language to comment on the political and media news as well as the many non-stories that set the internet ablaze every day. It took me some time to be able to describe what these sentences were like without euphemism – I mean, for these words to come out of my mouth in front of Dr Felsenberg, even if only to give some illustrative examples.

I refused to acknowledge that William was capable of conceiving and posting such horrors. And at the same time, it was as though I had always known.

And it's strange, the feeling of calm you get when finally it emerges, the thing you refused to see but knew was there, buried nearby; a feeling of relief when the worst is confirmed.

THÉO

The slight nausea suddenly gets worse. He lets his head slump into his hands. He knows he shouldn't – he should look into the distance, fix on a point in front of him – but he's curled up facing the cupboard and can't move. Under the canteen stairs, in their hiding place, there's no vanishing point to focus on. When he raises his eyes again, everything is pitching even more. He breathes slowly, steadily; he absolutely must not throw up. At that precise moment, nothing matters any more: not the fear of being noticed or of not being able to slide under the cupboard to get out. He just wants it to stop. He wants the vice crushing his skull to slacken its grip.

This morning he took an old bottle of Martini from his dad's that had almost a third left in it. The sugar had crusted around the neck and he had trouble getting the top off. On the metro he put his nose in his rucksack and just breathed in the smell. He'd enjoyed the smooth smell of the alcohol. He thought it would be easy to drink more than the last time.

He ate almost nothing in the canteen to get that immediate, stronger feeling of drunkenness when his stomach is empty. He's alone because Mathis has a Latin lesson. He waited until everyone had returned to their classes or the study room, then went to the staircase. He checked no one could see him, and slid into their hiding place.

The bell rings. Suddenly an intense din fills the corridors. Above the sound of voices and laughter, like an underground lake only he is aware of, he can hear sounds with unusual clarity: streams of students crossing paths, soles rubbing on the lino, clothes brushing, the displacement of air caused by this hourly migration: a ballet that he cannot see but whose every movement he feels. A wave of heat goes to his head. He needs to hold on a bit longer without throwing up before he can get out; wait until he's able to lie on the ground and crawl under the cupboard. But for now, he can't.

The corridors empty and the din dies away. He's going to be late for English. By now, Mathis will be getting worried. He didn't tell him he was going to their hiding place.

A thought flashes through his mind: no one knows he's here.

Now that silence has returned, he falls sleep sitting upright.

———

When he wakes, he has no idea what the time is. His mobile is dead, out of battery.

He could have been asleep for ten minutes or two hours.

What if it's evening? What if the school's locked up?

He listens. In the distance he can hear a loud voice coming from a classroom. He sighs with relief.

He's now capable of lying down without feeling as though his head is rolling away from him. In this position he continues breathing gently to contain the nausea. He slides onto his back, manages to get himself at the correct angle and wriggles under the cupboard. He only has a few millimetres to play with. He mustn't panic as his body passes under its bulk because there's almost no space above him.

He's managed to get out. The floor pitches as he walks. It's hard putting one foot in front of the other with this strange feeling that the ground is melting away at every step. He has to lean on the wall to make progress.

He looks at the clock. His English class will be over soon.

Mathis will be out shortly and will probably come looking for him.

When he goes into the toilets the feeling of nausea suddenly returns. He pushes open a stall. A ball of aluminium has formed under his tongue and he can't swallow it. His heart lurches, then his stomach spasms and he throws up a brown liquid into the bowl. A second, stronger jet almost makes him topple over.

The bell rings.

He has just enough time to splash water on his face and rinse his mouth out. Again the corridors are filling with the buzz of students changing class.

He grabs the washbasin to stop himself falling and his head begins to spin again.

He hears voices and laughter getting closer.

He goes back into the toilet cubicle. He doesn't want to see anyone.

He lets himself slide to the floor with his back against the wall, until he's in a half-sitting position that he can maintain, not too far from the toilet bowl.

When silence returns, he hears Mathis's voice.

Mathis is there. Mathis is looking for him. Calling for him.

HÉLÈNE

We were summoned by the Head – by 'we' I mean everyone who teaches Year 8 – to go over what happened. Mr Nemours could have made do with a face-to-face meeting with Éliane Berthelot and me, but as the altercation concerned Théo Lubin, and I'd already raised concerns about him, he decided to bring us all together.

He was keen to point out in front of the whole team that my behaviour had been completely out of line. In a school such as ours, such a lapse was unacceptable. Éliane Berthelot, who had initially threatened to make a complaint about me to the local authorities or even the police, had eventually changed her mind. She had demanded an apology, which I repeated in front of our assembled colleagues. Her little grimace of victory was quite a sight. Even if it in no way justifies my behaviour, I nevertheless asked that the punishment she had inflicted on Théo could be mentioned: is it appropriate to humiliate a thirteen-year-old boy by asking him to run in front of his classmates in pink Barbie jogging bottoms that are too small for him? Éliane Berthelot couldn't see any problem with that at all. Or to be more precise, she couldn't see how it was humiliating … According to her, Théo's repeated failure to bring his kit was pure provocation. He wanted to wind her up, as she put it. Frédéric spoke in my defence. His voice was firm, composed, a gentle demonstration of natural authority: there could be other explanations that were worth looking at. Especially as Théo had recently seemed tired, even disorientated, and voluntarily went to the sick bay.

Éliane Berthelot eventually admitted she wasn't keen on the boy, that she even felt dislike towards him. The Head, who was visibly displeased by this line of defence, pointed out that she was not required to like her students, merely teach them her subject and show fairness.

The others had kept out of it. When Mr Nemours asked their opinion, they all agreed that they hadn't noticed anything in particular, except that Théo Lubin was a very withdrawn student and it was hard to capture his attention. Nothing else. Éric Guibert mentioned that Théo had skipped his last class, though he'd been in school that morning. And in fact, thinking more carefully, unexplained absences in the middle of the day had happened several times. Frédéric spoke last and described seeing Théo crying one day when he played extracts from *The Magic Flute* to his class. Last, the nurse's report was read out by the

Head. Anyway, Mr Nemours encouraged everyone to be remain vigilant.

When the Head asked if any of us had been in contact with the parents, I felt panic. Without thinking, I said no like the others.

I then sensed Frédéric looking at me, incredulous. His mouth was half-open, but his eyes were fixed only on me, as if to say, *Why aren't you telling the truth, Hélène?*

The Head had looked up Théo's information sheet and noticed that the father's address didn't appear in any of his paperwork. He asked Nadine Stoquier, the chief education adviser, to try to get complete details for both parents.

The meeting ended there. No one had anything else to say.

When we left the office, Frédéric caught up with me. For a few seconds he walked beside me in silence. Then he put his hands on my shoulders (an instant shock, a brief electrical discharge, immediately absorbed by my body) to make me stop and listen.

'Why didn't you say you saw the mother?'

I didn't have an answer. Except that in the past few weeks, everyone around that table or outside of school, everyone I pass in the street, on the metro, or outside my building has become the enemy. Something inside me has woken up, that mixture of fear and anger that has lain dormant for years under the effect of an anaesthetic that resembles a mild drowsiness, whose dosage I've controlled myself, administered at regular intervals.

I've never experienced this feeling in such a brutal, invasive form, and the rage that I'm struggling to contain is stopping me sleeping.

No, I didn't say that I'd summoned the mother, though I'm risking the Head finding out soon and reprimanding me for lying to him; I'm risking him concluding, rightly, that I'm much too involved in this whole thing. It's true.

Frédéric's worried. He's afraid that the mother will come and complain about what I said. From her point of view, I summoned her without cause and alarmed her irrationally.

I wanted him to hug me. Let me rest the weight of my body against his for a few minutes. Lean on him. Breathe his smell, feel my back and shoulder muscles relax. Not, of course, for long.

When I left school I had no desire to go home. I walked aimlessly, dragged along by my own momentum, crossing the street now and then to avoid stopping. My anger had not diminished. It throbbed beneath my skin, in every part of my body. As long as I didn't detect any signs of exhaustion, I was unable to turn towards home.

I got back late and collapsed on my bed fully clothed.

CÉCILE

The other day Mathis surprised me in the kitchen. I hadn't heard him come in. He came up behind me.

'Are you talking to yourself, Mum?'

I was caught off guard.

'No, darling, I'm talking to the woman from downstairs, who's here but you can't see her.'

He puzzled for a moment, then laughed. Mathis has his father's sense of humour – when his father still had a sense of humour, that is. He opened some cupboards, looking for a snack, but he didn't seem to know what.

A little later, after some beating about the bush, he asked if he could invite Théo for a sleepover next weekend. I didn't know how to respond because on Saturday evening William and I have been invited out to dinner with friends and it would trouble me leaving the two of them alone. I said I'd think about it and talk to his father. I often say that: 'I'll talk to your father', but today the full absurdity of this phrase resonated. What is a thirteen-year-old boy to make of such a stupid statement? That I'm a wife who is subject to the wisdom of her husband? That masculine trumps feminine? That William decides everything? That I hide behind this authority, real or fictional, to avoid responsibility for my own decisions? That his father and I share everything? I felt pitiful.

Anyone who is or has been part of a couple knows that the other person is a mystery. I know it too. *Yes*, some part of the other escapes us, decisively, because the other is a mysterious being who guards his own secrets and dark, fragile soul. The other conceals about himself some remnant of childhood, his secret wounds; he tries to repress his confused emotions and obscure feelings. The other must, as we all must, learn to become himself and devote himself to a sort of self-optimisation. The unknown other cultivates his little secret garden. But of course I've known that for a long time; I wasn't born yesterday. I read books and women's magazines. Empty words, supreme platitudes that provide no consolation. Because I've never read that the unknown other – even the very one you live, sleep, eat and make love with; even the very one you believe you agree with, are in sync, even in harmony with – can turn out to be a stranger who harbours the vilest thoughts and utters words that spatter you with shame. What do you do when you discover that this part of the other who emerges from the void seems to have made a pact with the devil? What do you do when you realise that the back of your stage set is in fact immersed in a marsh that stinks like a sewer?

I shouldn't have picked up that ball of crumpled paper. I know that. I should have stayed in my gentle, blind ignorance, and kept talking to myself – for lack of alternative – to reassure, congratulate, calm myself.

But for how long?

The time of innocence is well and truly over. I can't stop myself going to look. Every morning, as soon as Mathis goes off to school and William to the office, I hurry to the computer. I start with his blog where he posts irregularly and then I make a tour of the sites and forums on which, by contrast, he posts comments almost daily. Sometimes even several times a day, when a discussion gets going and, in a vain display of competitive aggression, he reacts to others. On the web, Wilmor75 spreads his contempt and spews poison. In order to evade criticism, he uses contorted metaphors and clever insinuations. He knows how to tailor his words to suit the site he's on and doesn't ever seem to have been investigated.

I don't know the man who writes these words.

My husband isn't like that. My husband doesn't use that kind of language. My husband can't have within him the kind of stinking muck these lines exude. He's well brought up. He comes from a well-off, educated background. My husband doesn't spend his evenings spewing out torrents of filth to wallow in. My husband isn't the sort of man for mocking, yelling and vomiting on everything. My husband has better things to do. My husband isn't the man who shuts himself away almost every evening to let the fetid pus ooze from his wound.

My husband was funny, clever and handsome. I loved his composure and gift for repartee. He was a fine speaker. My husband was a flamboyant, generous man. My husband would tell me lots of stories, large and small. My husband was interested in other people's lives, including mine.

I try to explain to Dr Felsenberg the feeling of betrayal that takes hold of me in the middle of the night. Yes, William has betrayed me. William has hidden from me this part of himself that was spoiling for a fight, ready to destroy everything, who writes the opposite of what he thinks, or what he pretends to think.

Dr Felsenberg backs me into a corner. He asks if William knows everything about *my* life, *my* dark zones.

Of course not. But that's not the same.

'Oh, really?' he says, looking surprised.

'I'm not talking about a secret fantasy or a secret garden. I'm talking about cartloads of filth poured into a public place.'

'But maybe he's hiding them from you because he's ashamed?'

'Or maybe he thinks I'm too stupid to understand. Before this, William has never been shy of including me.'

'In what?'

'His little accommodations with reality.'

'Which ones?'

'The same sort that unite all couples, I imagine.'

'For example?'

He irritates me with his pretend questions. I answer him all the same.

'All couples abide by rules and customs, usually implicit ones, don't they? It's a sort of tacit contract that unites two people, however long that union lasts. I mean those more or less crude tricks that the two of you make without ever formalising them. Accommodations with reality – for example, with truth itself.'

'Meaning?'

'Well, for instance, at a dinner party, the husband will tell an anecdote about something that happened to them as a couple or a family: the amazing stroke of luck by which they met, the plane strike that began the day before their honeymoon, the storm of 1999 when they were driving their new car on a main road somewhere in the north, or when they found them-selves in a house with no water that was nothing like the one they'd rented from the travel website, or when their daughter fell off the big toboggan in the Parc de la Villette. So the husband is describing something they experienced together. And because he likes to make an impression, he embellishes a bit. Or goes further and adds some sensational details to make the story funnier, more gripping. He exaggerates, transforms. He assumes in doing so that his wife will make his lies her own. He assumes, rightly, that she will keep quiet and become his accomplice. And that's what she does.'

'Really?'

'Don't you? Do you contradict your wife in public when she tells a tiny fib?'

(I know Dr Felsenberg is married because he wears a wedding ring.)

He smiles. I pursue my train of thought.

'I think this tacit contract exists between every couple. To different degrees. Let's say the confidentiality clauses vary in length. And these exploits, revised to a greater or lesser extent, eventually construct a sort of family romance. An epic. Because after a time, you end up believing them.'

Dr Felsenberg remained silent.

Then I added this sentence, without knowing if it was the conclusion of what came before or the beginning of an argument I was yet to make.

'In fact, a couple is a partnership of malefactors.'

He waited a few seconds before starting again.

'The problem is that now you aren't part of it. And moreover, you don't want to be. Because this story is outside the contract. Ultimately, you could say that this time your husband didn't want to compromise you. He didn't seek your complicity.'

'That's true. But the problem is, I've seen it.'

He decided we would end the session there.

I'm starting to be familiar with his expert interruptions and cunning strategies. He's told himself that I'll cope on my own with my third-rate aphorisms and their hidden meanings. That those will get me there.

Yes, we're malefactors. Most likely. To one way of thinking. We negotiate relentlessly, practise concessions, compromise, we protect our offspring, obey the laws of the clan, we equivocate, simmer our little plans. But for how long? How long can you be the other person's accomplice? How far can you follow them, protect them, cover for them, act as their alibi?

That's the question Dr Felsenberg didn't ask. The one contained within my own words and which is bound to catch up with me in the end.

Yes, I love my husband. At least, I think I do.

But it has become so hard to love him.

Do people change that much? Do we all harbour something unnameable within us that is likely to reveal itself one day, as an ugly message in invisible ink would reveal itself in the heat of a flame? Do all of us hide a silent inner demon capable of leading a fool's existence for years?

I watch my husband at the dinner table and wonder: did the monster within him give a hint of his smell, his ways and the echo of his rage, which I didn't know how to recognise?

Am I the one who's changed? Am I the one who has turned him into this bitter creature full of bile?

MATHIS

He's not sure he finds it such fun any more.

At the beginning there was the shiver that ran through his spine, a faster heartbeat, a shot of adrenalin he felt spread through his whole body every time he and Théo managed to hide. Behind the cupboard they had an appointment with drunkenness. An excitement similar to the one he felt as a little boy when his mother took him to the merry-go-round and he climbed into the helicopter, which went up and down until he was dizzy.

But now he doesn't really want to any more. He's afraid he'll be seen, afraid of getting stuck behind the cupboard, of throwing up like Théo, of his mother finding out that he's been drinking again. He doesn't dare tell his friend he's scared. That he'd rather stop. Because that's all Théo's interested in: finding times when they can drink, escape attention, isolate themselves. Increase the measures, drink faster. The other games they invented or played together when they first met have been replaced by this game that Théo is playing against himself. Mathis misses the old days, when they swapped cards, shared comics, told each other about films or videos they loved. He doesn't really know any more how it began, how alcohol made its appearance. Maybe it was through Hugo the first time. Hugo had found the remains of a bottle his brother had left and hid it in his bag. They all took turns drinking and they laughed a lot.

Drinking was a game. At the start. A secret game the two of them shared.

Now it's all Théo thinks about. Mathis has barely set foot in the playground before he has to answer his friend's urgent questions: Has he found any money? Has he bought a little bottle? How much is left?

Two weeks ago Théo got a €20 note from his grand-mother. They ordered a big bottle of whisky from Hugo's brother, Baptiste, who still hasn't delivered it.

Today Ms Destrée has organised a trip to the Natural History Museum. She's decided to take them to the Evolution Gallery so that they can take part in the workshop on classifying living things.

This morning before leaving she took the register and then asked each student to send her their mobile number in case someone gets lost. They all left the school together and walked to the metro.

Théo isn't with them. Mathis is disappointed, but in the end he enjoyed the workshop a lot. By examining several animal species they worked out what attributes they have in common and the method scientists use to classify species.

He'd like to become a vet.

On the way back, as the class is walking to the school (there was no question of scattering into the wild, as the students had to be counted on their return from the trip), Ms Destrée asks him some questions. She wants to know why Théo doesn't take part in any outings.

Is he afraid of something? Has someone forbidden him to take part?

Mathis replies politely that he doesn't know.

As she allows the silence to go on, he feels obliged to add, 'Maybe he doesn't have the money.'

He'd really like to join the little group of girls walking just ahead of them, but Ms Destrée has no intention of letting him escape. She has more questions. She says she thinks Théo seems tired and sad. For a few minutes, Mathis wonders if she has noticed them, or if she suspects something, but what she wants to know is whether he's ever been to Théo's house, if he's met his parents. Mathis tries hard to reply as casually as possible, but he can tell how worried Ms Destrée is.

As they approach the school, with her still walking close beside him, now lost in thought, like someone searching for the solution to a mystery that's eluding her, he's on the point of coming straight out and saying, 'Théo's drinking alcohol like he wants to kill himself.' This sentence goes round in his head for several minutes: serious, solemn and impossible to say.

Rose suddenly catches up with them and almost as soon as she draws level asks if their next test will be about the trip.

Ms Destrée sighs. No, there won't be a test.

Mathis stays silent.

It's too late.

He should have said what he saw the day he went back to Théo's dad's with him.

It was the first time he'd been to the apartment.

Théo had never invited him up before, and every time he'd been to call for him, he'd stayed downstairs.

But this day Théo had slipped behind the cupboard on his own. He'd made himself ill with rum. In the end he'd come out and been sick in the school toilets. Mathis had found him there and helped him collect his things from his locker and then steered him down the stairs.

They took the metro together, stopping several times on the way because of the nausea, then they went slowly all the way to Théo's block. Once they were at the foot of the block, Théo tried to dissuade Mathis from going up with him, but he couldn't walk by himself. He had no other option than to tell him the entry code, floor and apartment number.

It was Mathis who put the key in the door. The apartment was in complete darkness, the curtains drawn. The smell caught his throat at once. The air was rancid, stale. The windows couldn't have been opened for a long time.

Théo called out, 'Dad, it's me. I'm with a friend.'

Mathis's eyes gradually became accustomed to the dark and he began to make out his surroundings. He had never seen such chaos. There were things scattered on the floor, all over the place, as though they had been abandoned there, in the middle of the room, in the passage, as though time had stopped. The table was covered in crumbs, empty yoghurt pots, piles of plates; bowls with dried-up liquids of different colours at the bottom sat beside the sofa; the remains of a pizza had hardened on a plate.

Théo began tidying up the things that were lying around, but his movements were clumsy and he almost broke a glass, so he stopped.

There was no point.

Théo's father appeared in the living room, barefoot and squinting as though getting used to a strong light, although the only light in the room came from the gap in the curtains. He was wearing some sort of loose trousers, though Mathis couldn't tell if they were pyjamas or tracksuit bottoms that sat low on his hips. He was like the caveman in the comic on human history that his grandmother had given him.

Mathis introduced himself politely the way his mother had taught him and then kept quiet. Théo's father scared him. He sat down at the table and looked at them, one after the other, without noticing the state his son was in. Mathis's mother, with her radar, would never have missed that.

'Everything OK, lads?'

Théo turned to Mathis and told him he could go.

He thanked him several times for coming up, having come all the way back with him, probably without meaning a word of it. He probably wished Mathis would disappear, or had never come. He felt ashamed and Mathis could sense that shame as though it were his own.

With his eyes lowered, Théo's father said nothing, frozen in a strange posture of reflection and withdrawal.

That was when Mathis noticed the gas cooker. One of the rings was on and turned up high, but there was no pan or casserole on it. From where he was, he could hear the gas burning as it fed the flame.

———

As he was about to leave, Mathis managed to look at Théo's father for several seconds and register the strange colour of his skin and his trembling hands. He mustn't forget a single detail. But why did this idea come into his head? Perhaps because of the flickering, pointless flame a short distance from them that no one seemed to see.

Mathis got up and said, 'Your gas is on ...'

Then Théo turned to his father and spoke to him as though scolding a child. 'Not again, Dad ... Were you wanting to make something to eat?'

Théo's father didn't reply. His gaze was lost in something vast and inaccessible and there was dried saliva at the corners of his mouth.

Théo went over to the cooker to turn it off. Apologetically, his father said, 'I was cold.'

Mathis asked if he could have a glass of water and his friend had to turn on the light. He came back and handed him the glass, which was dripping on the floor. His expression sealed a pact of silence between them.

Théo pushed Mathis towards the door. With a final thank you, he closed the door on him. Mathis still had the glass in his hand. He almost rang the bell, but in the end decided to leave the glass next to the doormat.

—

He headed back to the metro.

On his way, he remembered that when he was little and collecting pebbles with Sonia in the Bois de Vincennes, he'd say they were injured sparrows. He'd hold them carefully, stroke them with his fingertips, sometimes even talk to them to comfort them. He promised them they'd get better, grow bigger. He told them they'd soon be able to fly away. And when each pebble had absorbed the heat from his palm, when it seemed reassured, he'd put it in his pocket with the other pebbles he'd saved.

THÉO

Has his mother always been this thin-skinned woman from whom he keeps his distance, capable of changing her mood in a matter of seconds? He doesn't know. He's stopped snuggling against her when they're watching television, or giving her a hug when he says goodnight, or seeking the contact of her hand against his cheek. He's stopped kissing her. He has grown up and drawn away from her body.

Since she stopped crying, she always has this tense expression, pinched lips, watchful eyes. She's on her guard, ready to defend herself, to respond, to pick a quarrel. She never lets go. He rarely sees her laugh and when she does – as she did last week when one of her girlfriends came round for dinner – he's astonished by her face, which suddenly seems younger and gentler.

What he notices above all is the clot of hate his mother has kept within her, which has never been reabsorbed. He knows the clot is there and that all it takes is a few words for it to split in two and spread the black blood it contains. He knows that this hatred is the rotten fruit of a wound.

When he goes back to her house after a week at his father's, after he's put his things in the laundry basket and had a shower, once he's got rid of every trace of the enemy from himself, he can face her. And every time, at that precise moment, he wishes he could go over to her and, in a quiet voice, tell her everything. He wishes he could tell her how afraid he is for his father, how aware he is of the dark power that's crushing him and holding him down. He knows that every day his father is getting closer to a danger zone from which there is no return.

He wishes he could take refuge in his mother's arms. Calm himself in the cloud of her perfume. But he always encounters the stiffness of her back, arms by her sides, neck tense, her movements sharp and brusque. She can't enfold him. She has trouble looking at him. She's completely taken up with this: accepting into her domain the son who has returned from the detested land.

So this time, once again, he gives up.

He won't say anything.

It's OK. It'll work itself out. His father will get better. He'll help him.

Next week, he won't let himself be browbeaten. He won't allow crumpled paper and piles of bowls to be left lying around. He'll wipe the table and throw away the empty yoghurt pots.

And then he'll turn on the computer and look online for job ads for his father. He'll enter his selection criteria and call him to come and see.

Sometimes he wonders if being an adult is worth the trouble. 'Whether the game is worth the candle,' as his grandma would say. When she has to make an important decision, she fills columns with arguments 'for' and 'against', separated by a long line drawn with a ruler. When the question is about becoming an adult, are the two columns the same length?

Unlike most foods, alcohol is not digested. It goes direct from the digestive tract into the blood vessels. Only a tiny fraction of alcohol molecules are metabolised by enzymes in the intestine: that is, broken down into smaller fragments. The rest cross the stomach lining or the small intestine and immediately circulate in the blood. Within a few minutes, blood is transporting the alcohol to all parts of the body. They learned that in Ms Destrée's class.

The effects are felt quickest in the brain. Worry and fear recede and sometimes even disappear. They give way to a sort of dizziness or excitement that can last several hours.

But Théo wants something different.

He wants to reach the stage where the brain goes into standby mode. That state of unconsciousness. He wants the high-pitched noise that only he can hear to finally stop, the noise that wells up in the night and sometimes in the middle of the day.

For that, you need four grams of alcohol in the blood. At his age, probably a bit less. According to what he's read online, it also depends on what you eat and how quickly you drink.

It's called an alcoholic coma.

He likes these words, their sound, their promise: a moment of disappearance, obliteration, when you no longer owe anyone anything.

But every time he's come close, he's thrown up before he got there.

HÉLÈNE

There was a big fuss the other day at school. Apparently some students have been going behind the cupboard that blocks off the space under the canteen stairs. A cleaner found some scraps of paper that hadn't been there last week and she's certain couldn't have been thrown down from the stairs. According to what she said, this isn't the first time. The Head immediately took steps to block access. Two bags of cement have been slid under the cupboard. Firstly, the students are not supposed to escape our vigilance and secondly, if by chance one of them got stuck, it could be dangerous. When I was shown the scene of the crime, it had been made impossible to get through. I thought that you'd have to be slim and agile to slide underneath, and have a real urge to hide.

This is the kind of event that shakes up our small world for a few days. Everyone has their own interpretation and theories. We all need diversion.

———

That day, Frédéric waited for me after school. He wanted a word. On Tuesdays we finish at the same time. He told me he thought I seemed really tense and tired. He didn't know if it was this business that was putting me in this state or something else, something that my obsession had stirred up or that had caused it in the first place. He was the one who used the term 'obsession'. And I know him well enough to realise that he chooses his words with care.

A few years ago, Frédéric took me in his arms. We'd had a trying staff meeting. The two of us had clashed several times with the other Year 10 teachers. I was exhausted. Exhausted by seeing students steered towards paths which we knew full well would be dead ends for them just because places were available, or were low cost, or because we knew there was no chance that their parents would show up at school to kick up a fuss. I had said my piece several times in the meeting. I'd voiced astonishment, indignation, rebellion. I'd stuck my neck out and Frédéric had backed me up. We'd been successful in the case of three students, and avoided them having subject choices imposed on them by default, or out of laziness or resignation. When we left, Frédéric asked me for a drink. I accepted. I'd liked him for a long time, but I knew he was married. His wife has been seriously ill since the birth of their second child. That's what people still say to this day, in hushed voices, when he's not in the staffroom. And that he's not the type to dump a sick woman.

We had a few drinks to celebrate our tiny victories and after we had replayed the discussions from the meeting, with the inevitable impersonations, we began talking about our lives.

Late in the evening, in the street that led to the metro, Frédéric put his arms around me. We stayed like that for ages. I remember him caressing my hips, my buttocks and my hair. Through the flowing material of my floral dress, I felt his erection against my thigh. He didn't kiss me.

It could have been the start of an affair. Too dangerous for both of us. That's what he told me a few days later. That he didn't want to fall in love.

When I told friends about this, they laughed. Male excuse. Typical married man's get-out. That would probably have been true if we'd slept together. But we hadn't.

We have become solid, complicit colleagues. We share the same values, the same battles. Make a stand when that's all you can do. That's a start.

Frédéric knows me, it's true, even if our saliva never mingled. But he's wrong. I'm not the one people should be worried about.

CÉCILE

In view of the circumstances, I thought long and hard about going to this dinner with William. I was scared to think of standing beside him in public, letting people see us – or what's left of us – as a couple, being party to that pantomime. But I couldn't come up with a valid excuse to get out of it. We go out so rarely. That also happened gradually. We're invited out less and less often. We no longer go to the cinema. We never eat in restaurants. I don't know when the end of our social life dates from. As with many things, the fact is I'm unable to say when it began – to space out, dry up, die off – nor when it ended. Everything is happening as though I'm coming round from a strange torpor. From a general anaesthetic. And this question keeps on recurring: how could I have failed to realise sooner?

Previously – I mean, when we still used to go out – William always found something to criticise: people talked too much, took themselves too seriously, didn't ask questions. And he wasn't always wrong about that. We very rarely reciprocated the invitations. William doesn't like people coming to our home. I think he's afraid that allowing people to see the place we live, giving them access to our interior, will reveal our deception. Or, to be accurate, mine. He's afraid of the little detail, the faux pas that might escape his vigilance and reveal my background – a milieu where people don't just make errors in French, but also errors of taste. Some of which he's probably missed. It's not (of course) for want of trying to impose his ideas. And asking me to take things he thinks unworthy of our apartment down to the cellar. Besides, William has never liked entertaining. Even in the early days. He always did it grudgingly.

This time it was partly a work thing and my husband indicated that it was important to him. Charles, our host, also works for the group, but in another company. Anaïs, his wife, is a commercial law specialist. We've seen them two or three times, but they aren't friends. They moved a few months ago and were keen to have us round to their new apartment. So we set off around 8 p.m., leaving Mathis and Théo at home. In the end, our son had won easily: as we were going out, of course he got to invite a friend round rather than stay at home alone.

Anaïs and Charles had invited another couple we didn't know.

We sat around the coffee table drinking aperitifs. We swapped news and then, as always, I became invisible.

I'm used to this. Give or take a few details, the scenario is always the same. I'm generally asked two or three questions, and then after I've said that I don't work, the conversation shifts to someone else and never comes back to me. People don't imagine that a housewife can have a life, interests, still less anything to say. They don't imagine she can string together a few sensible sentences about the world around us or be up to formulating an opinion. It's as though the housewife is by definition under house arrest and her brain, having suffered oxygen deprivation too long, operates at reduced speed. Guests discover with a certain fear that they're going to have to put up with a person at their table who has withdrawn from the world and civilisation and who, apart from purely practical and domestic topics, won't be able to take part in any genuine conversation. So quite quickly I'm excluded from the company. They stop talking to me and, in particular, they stop looking at me. Mostly I let myself become absorbed by the colour of the walls or the pattern on the wallpaper. I look for vanishing points and I disappear.

In fact, for different reasons, William appreciates the fact that I'm a silent woman.

But this Saturday, over dinner, my husband began telling an anecdote. William has always liked to be the centre of attention. He likes the moment when silence descends around the table and all eyes converge on him and everyone shows signs of interest. It's a form of group allegiance. My mind was wandering, only vaguely following what he was saying. It was about a conference in the provinces and a very boozy dinner. They'd been hanging around outside with some colleagues, all of them pretty drunk, when a young woman they didn't know but who had taken part in the seminar walked past. One of them called out to her, as a joke.

The tone that William used about this woman snapped me out of the familiar, inner drifting state in which I'd taken refuge.

'… You can take it from me that she clenched her buttocks!' he was saying as I fully returned to the conversation.

Everyone laughed. Including the women. I'm always surprised that women laugh at jokes like these.

'Really?' I interrupted. 'She clenched her buttocks? Did that surprise you?'

I didn't give him time to reply. 'Do you want me to explain why?'

He was looking at the others, as if to say, *Look at the kind of woman fate has saddled me with.*

'Because you were four pissed blokes in a deserted business park, near some practically deserted Ibis or Campanile hotel. So yes, William, that's probably one of the essential differences between men and women, fundamental even: women have very good reason to clench their buttocks.'

An awkward silence had fallen. I saw William hesitate between getting me to explain exactly what I meant (at the risk that I would make a fool of myself in front of his friends if, for example, on the spur of the moment,

I came out with one of the turns of phrase he cannot bear) and dismissing my remark with a wave of his hand and going on with his story. He asked me, with barely a hint of condescension, 'What do you mean, my dear?'

(Need I add that William uses the expression 'my dear' to respond to women who contradict him on social networks or get enraged by what he has written? For example, he writes, '*My dear*, look around: most men are wimps' or, '*My dear*, go and get fucked in the ass by some Jew pharmacist. That's their speciality.')

I was addressing William, but also the other two men at the table.

'Do you clench your buttocks when you come across a group of young women who're manifestly drunk in the middle of the night?'

The silence was perceptibly deepening.

'Of course not. Because no woman, even if she's dead drunk, has ever put her hand on your penis or buttocks, or made a sexual remark when you've walked past. Because it's pretty unusual for a woman to throw herself on a man in the street or under a bridge or in a hotel room in order to penetrate him or force I don't know what into his anus. That's why. So yes, you should realise that any normal woman clenches her buttocks when she passes a group of four men at three in the morning. Not only does she clench her buttocks, she also avoids eye contact and any behaviour that might indicate fear, challenge or invitation. She looks straight ahead, is careful not to quicken her pace, and only starts to breathe again when she's alone in the lift.'

William watched me, astonished. I saw his mouth become a hard line and I thought that Wilmor probably had that expression when he was at his keyboard.

'My dear, don't talk nonsense. You never go out alone, especially not at night.'

'Perhaps it's not too late to start. Thank you for an excellent dinner, but I have to say I'm finding the conversation a little tedious. That's what you'll say to me in the car, isn't it? If I go home in two hours with you: "God, they're a pain in the arse!" Isn't it, *my dear?*'

A few minutes later I was in the street, alone and laughing.

For the first time, I had broken the rules. I had broken the pact with my husband. I have to admit that I replayed the scene in my head several times. Yes, yes, I know – talking to myself outside. Bursting out laughing, even! After all, lots of people talk to themselves. I walked for a bit before hailing a taxi. I was still laughing as I got into the back of the cab.

I spent the journey imagining how I'd describe this scene to Dr Felsenberg, which details I'd choose.

It's stupid, but I was so happy at the thought of finally having something to tell him.

I got back at half ten. They weren't expecting me so early.

I found them both sitting on the sofa in front of a reality TV show. At their feet were a bottle of whisky, two or three Coke cans and some plastic glasses.

They hadn't heard the key in the door. I came up behind them. They were completely euphoric, to the extent that Théo was virtually rolling on the floor – literally. I thought that something one of the characters in the programme had said must just have sent them into this state of competitive hilarity.

When Mathis finally realised I was there, I saw his face change, going in a flash from uninhibited laughter as a result of the alcohol to panic. The laughing stopped. Mathis started picking up the plastic glasses, removing evidence of the crime. Théo sat down again on the sofa. He wasn't in a fit state to do anything. Mathis seemed less drunk than his friend. That reassured me a little: on the disaster scale, we weren't the record holders.

I asked who had brought the alcohol.

Without hesitation, Théo said it was him.

He squared up to me a little defiantly, as though he was protecting Mathis, as though he had decided to take the brunt of my anger on his own, while Mathis was still fussing around, pretending to tidy up.

I asked him where he'd bought the bottle. How he'd paid for it. How much they'd drunk. Did his parents know he was drinking at the age of twelve and a half? I'd never spoken to a child this harshly. He stopped responding. I wanted to slap him and throw him out without more ado. Or take him in a taxi back to his house, but the truth was I was afraid he'd be sick in the car. He could barely stand.

Mathis tried to explain the fortuitous circumstances which had led them, against their will, to have this bottle of whisky, which had come into the apartment by itself, as it were, almost by breaking and entering (or some such nonsense), but I shouted, 'Go to bed, both of you!'

I didn't have to say it twice.

My son helped his friend down the hall and they disappeared.

I sat down where they'd been. A young woman in a swimming costume, with voluminous breasts, and make-up with colours and highlights that were rather fascinating, was talking to camera. I paused to listen – maybe she knew some truth that had escaped me – but I heard her chuckle, 'Let's shake some booty,' and switched off the television.

I poured myself a generous measure of whisky in an empty glass and downed it in one. I wanted to laugh again.

THÉO

He wasn't afraid when she came in, unexpectedly, right in the middle of the evening. He just thought it was much too early and that because of her, yet again, he wouldn't be able to go all the way.

He wasn't afraid either when she asked him all those questions, a real police interrogation. She wanted details.

He knows how to keep quiet. He really didn't care that Mathis's mother was furious or that she sent them to bed like little boys.

But he was scared when she appeared in the room at nine o'clock the next morning and announced she was taking him home. She knew he was at his father's this weekend and of course wanted to speak to him. She had some things to tell him. It was important for parents to keep each other informed, she said. She couldn't say nothing about something so serious, he needed to understand that. She said she was sorry, but she didn't look at all sorry. She looked like someone who was bored and had just found something to occupy herself. She told him to have a shower and get dressed while she made breakfast.

Sitting in front of his bowl of hot chocolate, Théo claimed that his father worked on Sunday mornings and wouldn't be home. But she wasn't going to be taken in.

'Give me his number so that I can confirm that with him.'

'He doesn't have a mobile and the landline isn't working.'

'In that case we'll have to go and see him.'

He wasn't hungry. His whole body felt knotted. All the organs they'd drawn in biology had got tangled up and now formed a compact, painful ball.

She wasn't going to change her mind, he could be certain of that.

She insisted that he finish his bowl of hot chocolate. It was very cold outside and she didn't want him going out on an empty stomach. She was making an effort to speak nicely to him. Her voice sounded false.

He knows that Mathis's mother doesn't like him.

He doesn't like her either. She uses weird expressions when she speaks, which she must have copied from old books. She speaks as though French were a foreign language that she had learned off by heart or had borrowed from someone.

He forced down the hot, milky drink. Across the table, Mathis was looking at him helplessly. He was searching for a way to prevent his mother from going with him, but no ideas were coming.

She indicated that it was time to go and went to get Théo's jacket from the cupboard. (At Mathis's everything is tidied away. Everything has a place that has to be respected.) As she handed it to him, she expressed surprise that he wasn't dressed more warmly.

She didn't want Mathis to go with them. She knows Théo's father lives somewhere around the place d'Italie. She looked at the metro map to check how to get there. She told Théo he'd have to show her the way when they came out of the station.

On the way down in the lift, he retied his shoelaces so as not to have to look at himself in the mirror or meet this woman's eye.

Now she's walking beside him, authoritative and brisk.

Théo feels his heart beating in his stomach in the place where the alcohol first warms and then calms him.

She mustn't cross the threshold. She mustn't enter his father's apartment, let alone talk to him.

If she crosses the threshold, it's all over.

By any means at all, he must keep her away. Prevent her from getting near.

They're heading towards the metro. He matches his pace to hers. She senses him following her stride. Then her vigilance relaxes for a few seconds and Théo seizes this brief moment to make a run for it.

He pelts along the boulevard de Grenelle, runs without looking back, keeps going past the first station on Line 6 in case she catches up with him and runs even faster to the next.

At Sèvres-Lecourbe he takes the stairs four at a time to get to the overhead metro. He's laughing. At the last moment he leaps into a carriage just as its doors are about to shut.

That was close!

Rooted to the spot, she was! Didn't know what hit her.

HÉLÈNE

The other day when I announced that we would start studying reproduction after the holidays, Rose interrupted me.

'Do you have children, Miss?'

I said no and went on with the lesson. Usually, with the students I extricate myself from these situations with a little joke. But not this time.

I took the blows and I kept the secret right to the end. I'm thirty-eight and I don't have children. I don't have any photos to show, or names and ages to announce, no anecdotes or funny remarks to relate.

I'm sheltering within me the child I will never have, though no one knows it. My ruined stomach is inhabited by faces with diaphanous skin, tiny white teeth and silky hair. And when I'm asked the question, asked if I have children – which happens whenever I meet someone new (particularly women), after I've been asked what I do (or just before) – each time I have to resign myself to drawing the white chalk line on the ground that divides the world in two (those who have, and those who don't), I want to say: no, I don't have any, but look in my belly at all the children I haven't had; look at them dance to the rhythm of my steps – all they ask is to be cradled; look at this love, which I have retained, transformed into ingots; look at the energy I haven't expended, which I still have to expend; look at my innocent, wild curiosity and my appetite for everything; look at the child I have remained because I couldn't become a mother, or by virtue of that.

A long time ago a man left me because I couldn't have children. Now every night he lingers in his office and goes home as late as possible to avoid seeing the ones he has.

When I wake in the night, this question often returns. Why didn't I say anything? Why did I let the Wheel of Fortune turn without telling anyone, without calling for help? Why did I let my father persist with the quizzes, the traps and the kicks? Why didn't I cry out? Why didn't I report him? 'Right, Hélène, time to concentrate. A history question next or, rather, psychology.

Why did you keep your trap shut? What a pity, Hélène, you could have doubled your stake.'

But deep down, I know.

I know that children protect their parents and that the pact of silence sometimes leads to their deaths.

Today I know something that other people don't. And I mustn't close my eyes.

Sometimes I tell myself that that's the only point of becoming an adult: to repair what was lost and damaged at the start. And to keep the promises of the child we once were.

I didn't take Frédéric's advice. I continue to come to school and watch Théo. Standing by the window, as soon as the students go out into the playground, I try to pick him out. If I manage to spot him among the others – magnetised bodies, brought together by strange alliances – I spend the break spying on his movements, his dodges, looking for an answer.

On some pretext or other, I consulted the information forms the students filled in at the start of the year. I found his mother's address there.

I went to his neighbourhood several times. I don't know what I was looking for. Maybe to bump into Théo away from school, seemingly by accident, so that he could talk to me. I kept getting closer to the building, inside an ever-smaller perimeter. One evening I even stood on the pavement opposite for several minutes, looking up at the lighted windows.

The other day, just I was passing his building, someone tapped in the entry code and went in. I followed him. I found myself inside without intending to. Names and floor numbers were displayed on an information panel in front of the letter boxes. I didn't stop to think. I took the stairs to the third floor. As I approached, my heart was pounding so hard I could scarcely breathe. The apartment was silent; I couldn't hear any noise. Then suddenly the door opened and I found myself face to face with Théo's mother. (It would probably be more accurate to say that she found herself face to face with me.) I think our eyes met for the tiniest fraction of a second, and then I hurried down the stairs. I should have come up with some excuse, a reason to justify my presence. I could have pretended to have friends in the same building. Yes, what a coincidence! And claim that I'd got the wrong door, but it was too late: I was in the street and running as fast as I could.

THÉO

When he got home that Sunday, he found his father lying in his bedroom with the curtains closed. He went gingerly towards him, letting his eyes grow accustomed to the darkness. When he reached the bed, he saw that his father wasn't asleep. He seemed to be waiting for something, his arms motionless on top of the sheet, his upper body propped up on pillows. He was staring at a point on the wall that only he could see. He looked at Théo for a few seconds, as though he needed time to recognise his son, then a few seconds more to be able to adopt the appropriate response. For a brief moment his face registered that fleeting spark of joy that used to animate it when he collected Théo from primary school, and then he put his hands beneath the sheet. He asked Théo if he'd had fun. He repeated the question several times. It wasn't a polite formula, it was a real question, and the answer mattered to him.

Théo replied that it had all gone really well. There was a short silence during which he couldn't help wondering if Mathis's mother might have followed him or might soon find his address and turn up without warning.

For the first hour, he listened out for the noise of the lift and froze every time he heard the sound of a voice on the stairs.

Later, he spent the afternoon tidying and cleaning in case someone came. A sort of intuition told him that that was the most important thing to do, restore some order to his father's apartment.

It wasn't all that complicated. His father had taught him the trick of turning chores into a game, back when he was still capable of laughing and staying out of bed for more than four minutes. To transform the most boring task into a paper chase or a treasure hunt, all you had to do was set a target or a challenge, or invent a story.

This time Théo imagined he was taking part in a famous reality TV show. He was being tracked by about ten cameras all over the apartment that were broadcasting *The Big Clean-Up* challenge live. At the very moment he was filling the basin with water, more than a million people were following his actions. Because he was the youngest contestant in the whole history of the game and definitely the viewers' favourite. The day's challenge was particularly long and tough, but might enable him to win victory. Like the others, he would be scored at the end of *The Big Clean-Up* both on his speed and efficiency. And he is, in both categories, the best.

An imaginary voice-over eagerly commented on his actions, highlighting their agility and precision. This evening, in the diary room, he'll be able to tell the camera how he felt during the task, the moments of doubt, and the determination that nonetheless never left him. And with a bit of luck, he'll soon be on the cover of all the TV magazines.

His father hasn't got up since Sunday. For three days he's been dozing in bed. The door has stayed half-open but he never opens the curtains. He only gets up to go to the toilet, dragging his feet; Théo hears the sound of his slippers shuffling over the parquet, and then the noise of the flush. He hasn't had a shower and has eaten practically nothing. Théo brings him water in a carafe and makes him little sandwiches, which he barely touches.

Théo could tell his grandma, but he doesn't know her number. And anyway, she doesn't come round any more. The last time, which is already several months ago, she had an argument with his father. As she was leaving, she turned to Théo with a fake look of surprise and said, 'You're so like your mother.'

———

A plastic bag on the kitchen dresser with the logo of the local pharmacy contains the medicine his father takes every day. During the night, Théo takes the boxes out of the bag and reads the instructions.

In biology, Ms Destrée told them about molecules that have an effect on the brain. She explained how doping in sport works and why it's banned. Then she talked about medicines that can change a person's mood, help them to be less sad, less anxious, and sometimes even restore the reason of people who do and say crazy things. But these are dangerous medicines that only a psychiatrist or a doctor can prescribe.

But Théo's father has a heap of medicines, boxes and boxes, though he never leaves the apartment. It's as if he's stockpiled them for months.

Perhaps Théo could go and see Ms Destrée and talk to her about his father.

Sometimes when she's drawing on the board with chalk or explaining all the things that go on inside an organism, he has the impression that she's talking to him. Perhaps she knows. And can keep a secret.

CÉCILE

Now I'm scared. Scared that something will happen to us. I'm imagining horrors, I can't help it. I construct catastrophe scenarios, gruesome sequences of events, tragic coincidences. Every night when I go to bed, it occurs to me that I may not wake up. A mass presses down on the left side of my chest and stops me breathing. Or else I notice a diffuse pain in the pit of my stomach and suddenly feel afraid that my body's damaged flesh is host to one of those invasive cancers that's about to declare its presence.

My children are too young to lose their mother. That's what I'm thinking just as I close my eyes.

Dr Felsenberg calls these 'morbid thoughts'.

They reveal, he says, an old sense of guilt.

It's gruelling. It's a spiral that sucks me in, absorbs me, and against which I'm powerless. The morbid thoughts can crop up at any time, as images or words. When I try to describe them, they lose their texture, their heat, they no longer seem so tangible. They appear as what they are: constructs produced by anxiety, distant, hypothetical threats. But in the moment, they stop me breathing.

The temperature has suddenly plummeted. There's been a frost for several nights in a row. Gritters criss-cross the city before dawn to prevent ice forming. At first I thought that the cold might cleanse everything, eliminate the germs, bacteria, vermin, eradicate all the invisible filth we're surrounded by, and then the cold itself became a sly, insidious danger, another distinct threat in my hideous night thoughts.

I didn't say anything to William about Mathis. Probably because I'm sure this comes from me. Perhaps more generally the problem comes from me. I'm the defective cog hidden within a middle-class machine that has worked since the dawn of time. I'm the grain of sand that jams the mechanism, the drop of water that inadvertently falls in the fuel tank, the black sheep dressed up as a homemaker. My deception is at the root of this disaster. I dreamed of a cosy family apartment that I could go into raptures about. I dreamed of bright-eyed children raised in an atmosphere of kindness and comfort. I dreamed of a peaceful life centred around their education and my husband's well-being. I didn't ask for more than that and I stuck with it. I thought that would be enough. Keep a low profile, do the vacuuming and make the tea. Let there be no misunderstanding: I am where I wanted to be. Nonetheless, I've veered off course. Perhaps I used to be a seagull trapped in an oil slick, but now I'm strangely like the crow in the story my grandmother used to tell me, the coarse bird with the jet-black plumage who dreamed of being a white bird. Because this is how the fable goes: the bird first rolls in talcum powder, then flour, but the trick doesn't last long and soon it's gone. So then he dunks himself in a pot of white paint, in which he gets trapped. I am that black bird who wanted to become white and who betrayed his own kind. I thought I was smarter than that. I thought I could imitate the call of the turtle doves. But I too have lost the use of my wings, and where I am now, struggling is useless.

I can't speak to William any more. I just can't.

The longer I spend looking at what he writes on the internet – traces that will never be erased, lasting imprints that some day will reveal the deformity of the monster – the less I'm able to talk to him. My husband has become a stranger.

I'd like to be able to forget what I've read. To ignore the swamp surrounding us, which will soon invade our living room. Not to turn on the computer. But I can't.

Yet every day that goes by, I create a new lie, much bigger than the ones that made me and William second-class crooks who were never unmasked. I keep quiet and continue to fight the dust and carefully turn the dial on the washing machine, plug in the food mixer and the iron, change the sheets and wash the windows, leaving no smear visible, even in bright sunlight.

Which is the real William? The one who disseminates his bitter prose under the cloak of anonymity or the one who goes around with his face visible in a dark-grey suit, suavely tailored at the waist? The one who wallows in the mire or the one who wears immaculate white shirts carefully ironed by his wife?

I must tell my husband that I know.

Maybe these two parts of him will join to make just one? Perhaps I could establish a link between the two entities? Perhaps then I'd understand something that's eluding me?

Sometimes I think of that ball of crumpled paper, abandoned in the wastepaper bin. I wonder if, without realising, William was hoping that his double would be discovered, thwarted and jeered at, and at last someone would send him to the dungeon in handcuffs.

———

I need to find a solution for Mathis. I don't want him keeping company with Théo. Yes, I say 'keeping company with', like my mother did, so there you go. I don't want him coming home from school with him or sitting beside him in class. I'm sure that boy is having a harmful, unhealthy influence on our son, apart from the fact he's leading him to drink.

I've requested a meeting with their form teacher Ms Destrée through the school's website.

I'll talk to her. I'll explain.

And then at the end of the academic year, we'll send Mathis to a new school if we have to.

THÉO

Don't tell your mother that Sylvie has gone. Don't
tell your mother that Dad no longer has a job. Don't tell
your mother that Grandma Françoise is angry. Don't
tell your mother the sink is leaking. Don't tell your
mother I've sold the car. Don't tell your mother we can't
find that sweatshirt. Tell your mother we're not sure
yet what we're going to do. Tell your mother I'm waiting
for a rebate and I'll be able to pay for your lunches soon.
Don't tell your mother we didn't go out. Tell your mother
we couldn't have a meeting. Don't tell her that …

When he shuts his eyes, he sometimes sees their faces
the way they used to be, like in the photo where they're
together, smiling. His mother has long hair. She's turning towards his father, who's looking at the lens. He's
wearing a short-sleeved polo shirt. He has his arm
round her waist. This photo used to comfort him. Now
he knows that photos are just another sort of hoax.

MATHIS

He'd like to go back. Back to when he was small, when he spent hours building things with little pieces of plastic, when all he had to do was make houses and cars and planes, and all sorts of creatures with moving limbs and amazing powers. He remembers a time that doesn't seem so long ago – almost close enough to touch, yet definitely gone – a time when he played at Guess Who? and Whack-a-Mole with Sonia on the living-room carpet.

It all seemed simpler to him back then. Perhaps because beyond the walls of the apartment and the school, the world was abstract: a huge place meant for adults that didn't concern him.

Access to the place under the canteen staircase has been blocked. They don't have anywhere to hide any more. This gave Mathis a feeling of relief that he couldn't have explained, but Théo very soon began looking for another safe place away from all surveillance. Hugo told them about a garden near the Esplanade des Invalides that you could get into easily when it was closed.

This morning, while they're waiting for the first bell, Hugo comes over to them looking conspiratorial. If he were a bit taller and stronger, Mathis would have told him to get lost even before he opened his mouth, but he's known for a long time that he doesn't have the sort of physique that makes sudden outbursts possible. Of course, Hugo still didn't have the bottle that Théo ordered. But he did have some good news: his brother Baptiste was organising a party on Saturday. There would be quite a few of them, outdoors, and there would be plenty to drink. Excitedly he kept repeating, 'Enough to get really pissed!'

The meeting place was in front of the Santiago du Chili gardens at exactly 8 p.m. Baptiste would show them how to scale the gates without getting spotted. Once inside, they'd have to stay alert and be ready to hide because a park attendant sometimes did his rounds in the evening. And there was no need to worry about the cold; the gin would warm them up.

Mathis has been thinking about it constantly since this morning.

He has absolutely no desire to go. And anyway, he can't. Given what happened last time, when his parents went out to dine with friends, his mother won't be prepared to let him go out.

If it were just up to him, he'd say no. Baptiste and his friends kept Théo's money to buy an extra bottle and now they're bossing them around. He doesn't like that. They haven't kept their word.

He wishes Théo had refused to go. But his friend said yes and has already worked out his plan: he'll say he's sleeping at Mathis's. There's no risk of his father phoning to check. And nothing else matters. He'll be in control of his time and his movements: a whole evening of freedom. When Mathis expressed concern about where he would really sleep, Théo just said, 'We'll see.'

Mathis would like to keep out of this whole thing, stay at home and know nothing about it. But he can't leave Théo alone with them.

He's going to have to find a way to be there. He'll have to lie. Find an unbeatable reason for his mother to let him go out despite 'what happened', because that's the way she refers to it, in a low voice.

She hasn't said anything to his father.

He needs to think.

In fact, lying isn't difficult when it's for a good reason. The other day, for example, when she came back barely ten minutes after they left, furious at Théo for giving her the slip under the overhead metro, Mathis swore that he didn't have his friend's address – neither his father's nor his mother's – and didn't know how to get there either.

The week after, he went down to the cellar with his mother to look for a box that she was hoping contained some of her old things. While they were down there, she had a word with him. She told him she didn't want him to see Théo or sit beside him in class. She was expecting him to stay away from Théo and make friends with other boys in his class. It was out of the question that Théo would set foot in their house again or that Mathis would go to his.

He hardly recognised her voice, it was so firm and brooked no appeal. It was not up for discussion. It was an order and she wanted him to comply.

His mother's been strange for a while. She talks to herself without realising. She no longer seems sad in that way that made him so uncomfortable, or has the dejected look that sometimes surprised him; now she seems busy, run off her feet. The other day he saw her in the distance in the street. She was muttering to herself. You'd have thought she was crazy.

HÉLÈNE

On Thursday afternoon Théo stayed behind at the end of my class. He waited for all the others to leave. It was the last lesson of the day. I'd just finished the chapter on brain activity and how the nervous system works, which I usually spend two or three periods on. I saw he was taking his time putting his things away. Mathis left before him. I think he has singing or a piano lesson on Thursdays, so he never hangs around.

When we were alone, Théo came towards me. He was standing tall, jacket fastened, chin raised, his bag over his shoulder. I thought, he's got something to tell me. I held my breath. I mustn't force things or try to rush them. I smiled at him and pretended to be tidying the papers scattered over my desk. After a moment, he asked, 'Can you die if you take the wrong medicine?'

My pulse quickened. There was no room for error.

'You mean if you take medicine that's not intended for you?'

'No, not that.'

'What then?'

'Well … if someone takes medicine that doesn't work. You said that medicine works on the brain. On people's mood. But I think that sometimes it doesn't do anything. And people stay in bed. They hardly eat and they don't get up and they stay like that all day.'

He said this very quickly. I needed to decipher it and ask the right questions.

'Yes, that's true, Théo. That does happen. Are you thinking of someone in particular?'

He looked up at me. I could see his pupils dilate in response to the pressure.

Just then, the Head burst into my class without knocking. I turned to him, stunned. I didn't have the chance to open my mouth before he ordered Théo to go home in a tone that clearly suggested he had no business being there. Théo cast me a final glance, his eyes dark and accusing, as though I were a bank employee who had secretly pressed the panic button under the counter.

He left without looking back.

I followed Mr Nemours to his office.

Calmly and with a slightly theatrical firmness, he set out the situation for me.

Théo Lubin's mother had phoned to complain. Not only had I called her in for no reason, but now, she said, I was loitering around near her home. Even in her building. Of course, she'd related the conversation we'd had a few weeks back, which she'd called unfair and accusatory. The Head asked her to recall the exact tenor of what I said, which she'd had no trouble doing, judging by the detailed report he set before me.

Besides breaking the school rules and exceeding my remit, I'd failed to mention this encounter at the team meeting about the student. A meeting organised, did he have to remind me, after a first transgression on my part. Why had I said nothing? That was a mistake. A serious mistake. My behaviour was damaging the smooth functioning of the public education service and harming that service's reputation.

Théo's mother had asked for him to be moved to another class. The Head had told her he would speak to me so that I could explain myself and then make a decision.

He waited for my reaction. My argument. My justification. What on earth was I doing on those stairs? I had nothing to say in my defence, so I stayed silent. Fortunately, he didn't have punishment in mind. He's been teaching for over twenty years. He knows the pressure, the stresses that we're under and the responsibilities we bear. We need to stay united. Stick together. In view of the work I'd done in the school over several years, he wouldn't be calling for an official reprimand or warning. However, he told me I needed to put things in perspective and get myself signed off by a doctor. For at least a month. To let everyone calm down. That was a condition; it wasn't up for discussion.

———

I emptied my locker and left school with the disturbing conviction that I wouldn't be going back.

The music from *Wheel of Fortune* was going round in my head, 'I'll buy an A, I'll offer an L, I'll buy a C'; I'm near the target, I need to think to crack it, to find the right answer. 'Oh no, Hélène. Come on. It's not that simple. Who do you think you are? You weren't thinking that you could change the direction of the Wheel, were you?'

I haven't listened to the messages my colleagues have left on my machine throughout the day.

I haven't called Frédéric, who's tried phoning several times.

From my window I'm watching the passers-by wrapped up in their coats, hands in their pockets or protected by gloves, their shoulders hunched, hurrying and struggling against the damp air that cuts through their meagre defences. Among them there's a woman wondering how long an onion tart needs in the oven, another has just decided to leave her husband, another is mentally calculating how many luncheon vouchers she has left, a young woman is regretting having worn such thin tights, another has just heard that she's got the job after several interviews, and an old man has forgotten why he's there.

CÉCILE

The good thing about talking to yourself is that you can tell yourself jokes. I know some good ones that my brother used to tell me when we were children. They had us rolling on the floor with laughter.

The other day I was amusing myself talking in an English accent to myself. It was funny. I must say I can put it on rather well. It's crazy how much that enables you to take the drama out of a situation. It's a bit like Jane Birkin taking it upon herself to comfort me. But it's me and me alone who was talking to me, of course. And yes, out loud in my living room. I reviewed pretty much every topic.

I told Dr Felsenberg about that. He wanted to know from whom or from what the English accent estranged me.

My father died a long time ago and Thierry eventually left home. Since then, my mother has lived in a little ground-floor flat on staircase G in the building we grew up in. The council gave her a two-bedroom instead of the four-bedroom we used to live in, which means she can pay the rent and live decently. She's not the complaining sort.

I called her the other day. I didn't stop to think, I just picked up the phone and dialled her number. She was surprised; I don't call often. I told her I wanted to hear her voice, to get her news. There was a short silence and then she asked if everything was OK. I said yes, and then there was silence again. My mother never asks me specific, direct questions. I live in a world that seems too distant from hers. I know that Sonia goes to see her from time to time. My mother serves tea and biscuits that she arranges in a circle on a little plate. Then she puts them in a box so that my daughter can take them away with her. I said I'd go and see her with Mathis one day soon. After another pause, my mother said, 'OK, I'll be expecting you,' as though there were nothing else to hope for from life between the moment a promise is made and its fulfilment.

Ms Destrée hasn't responded to my request for a meeting. I think that's a bit much. She's supposed to be the contact for Year 8 but doesn't reply when it comes to seeing parents outside those interminable parents' meetings twice a year. I logged on to the school website several times and re-sent my message. In the end I rang them. They told me she was ill but not how long she'd be away. I hope I can see her as soon as she's back.

On the surface, nothing has changed. William has never referred to the dinner party with his friends. In his eyes it's probably just a minor incident. A mood swing. He must have got himself out of it with some fancy footwork, then refilled his glass. I'm not sure whether William has noticed my body has distanced itself from his. We haven't made love for several weeks, but this isn't the first time. He must be telling himself that I'm going through one of those dark phases that punctuate women's lives. Something hormonal probably, since that's the prism through which he observes the female sex, going by Wilmor's writing.

To be honest, I've stopped looking. I no longer turn the computer on since discovering that my husband has also started a Twitter account, which allows him to comment in a more incisive format and even slyer way on everything and nothing without ever assuming responsibility for the content of his remarks. It's a funny world that lets us pour out anonymous opinions all over the place, ambiguous or extreme, without ever identifying ourselves.

The very next evening after that dinner, William sat down close to me on the sofa. He put his arm around my shoulders. I felt my body stiffen; the contact of his palm burned my skin through the fabric. He told me he still had some work to do, he was sorry – it was a complicated report he had to send the head of his department the next day.

I looked at him for a few seconds, silently at first, and then asked, 'Are you sure there's nothing you want to tell me?'

He laughed, that nasal laugh that sometimes hides his embarrassment. He sensed that the question was not inconsequential. That it exceeded the framework of daily domestic interactions to which our conversations have been reduced. William isn't stupid. He stared at me enquiringly. He was waiting to see what was coming next. I asked him again.

'Are you sure you've nothing to tell me ... about you, about what you're doing?'

I couldn't say more. I didn't have the strength. But I'm certain that at that moment he understood.

He hesitated.

A tenth of a second.

I saw it because, though I don't know Wilmor, I do know William very well: a tiny twitch of his eyelids, the way he clasps his hands, the little embarrassed cough that lets him put an end to a conversation.

Then he stroked my cheek, furtively, a gesture from before, from a very long time ago: before the children, before computers, mobile phones, before the spider on the web.

He stood up. He was already turning away when he answered, 'You're imagining things.'

William shut himself in his office. I watched a TV documentary about mass-produced pizzas. It was about the flavouring agents and condiments added to mask the poor quality of the toppings, a trick revealed at the end of a big investigation carried out against a backdrop of mafia codes of silence and dramatic music. A real thriller. I really couldn't have cared less, but I watched it to the end. The Sunday before I'd watched one about coconuts. Since when have peak-time documentaries been about things like kittens and mince?

I talked to myself for a few minutes. I needed to debate. My voice no longer limits itself to reassuring me. Now it also expresses opinions.

Through the door I told William I was going to bed. I tidied a couple of things that were lying around the kitchen and drew the curtains in the living room.

Then I went through the bedtime routine (make-up remover, orange-blossom water, night cream, hand cream) in a sort of ritual that I imagine all women of a certain age have.

I lay down. I turned out the light and this phrase came to my mind as clearly as if I'd said it aloud: *I want to get out.*

MATHIS

This evening he's waited until his father has shut himself in his study and his mother is on her own in the living room. He's well prepared.

He takes one last breath.

'You know, on Saturday we're going to the Philharmonic with Mr Châle.'

She's surprised, as he expected.

'Oh really? Since when? Haven't you already been?'

'No, that was the opera. Don't you remember? It was on that form you filled in a while ago. You even gave me the money.'

'And where is this form?'

'I gave it back to Mr Châle because he has to keep all the parents' consent forms.'

She stops for a moment (she's spent the past two days sorting through things as though they were on the point of being evicted from their apartment). Mathis feels dozens of insects swarming in his stomach. He can only pray she doesn't hear them.

His mother looks puzzled. But he's ready for all her questions.

'On a Saturday night?'

'Yeah, because the school managed to get tickets because a group of pensioners cancelled. Mr Châle said it was a great opportunity, even if the seats are a long way from the stage.'

'The whole class?'

'No, just the ones who take music.'

'And what are you going to hear?'

'The Grand Orchestre de Paris. Henry Purcell and Gustav Mahler.'

He's prepared the details: how they'll go, how they'll return, which teachers are in charge of the trip. His mother is the sort of mother who is prepared to believe that they would have a trip to the Philharmonic on a Saturday evening.

Lying is really easy. He even experiences a certain pleasure in overdoing it. He puts on his good-little-boy voice.

'Ms Destrée was supposed to come with us, but it's going to be someone else because she's ill.'

Strangely, this detail seems to reassure his mother and establish the credibility of what he's saying.

She says she'll come and collect him after the concert so that he doesn't have to make his own way home. He begs her not to. He'll feel embarrassed, look like a baby.

The others will make fun of him. Mr Châle has said he'll bring back the students who live near the school so as not to inconvenience parents who have plans for the evening.

Eventually she gives in and he has the impression she's already thinking about something else, or doesn't have the strength to pursue her investigations any further. For several days she's been like someone leading a secret life that's very hectic and very tiring.

A little later, just as he's about to turn out his light, she comes in to his bedroom.

She asks him a question, direct and unexpected. 'Tell me, Mathis, you're not making things up?'

Without a second's hesitation: 'No, Mum, I swear.'

THÉO

The cold has covered the city in tissue paper. An incredibly fine white powder has come down on the lawns of the esplanade in front of Les Invalides. The benches are empty and the wind has chased away any passers-by.

They meet at exactly 8 p.m.

Baptiste told them to wait at the street corner, close to the entrance to the gardens, in front of a no entry sign.

They wait for his signal.

One by one, with the same alert, silent movement, they scale the gates and disappear into the bushes. A first stop, just long enough to make sure they haven't been seen.

After a few minutes, they set off again towards the back of the gardens. In single file, following Baptiste.

Behind the trees there's a small empty space. On the ground the shape of an old sandpit is visible, now filled in with earth. Baptiste tells them to sit in a circle with gaps between them so that they can play a game.

———

Baptiste and his friends have brought several Oasis bottles in which they've mixed gin and fruit juice. Half and half. He suggests a first round to get them going and hands out plastic glasses.

It's sugary and strong at the same time. Théo downs his in one. His eyes start to water but he doesn't cough.

He waits for the wave of heat to spread across his shoulders and down his spine.

Quentin laughs, surprised that Théo can down it like that at his age.

Baptiste gives them some advice: they can't sit still for too long because of the cold. They need to stand up regularly and jump on the spot and clap their hands to keep warm.

Théo says nothing. He's waiting for the feeling of heat within him, which is slow in coming. He watches the others. Mathis is pale. He looks scared. Maybe because he lied to his mother. Hugo is sitting beside his brother, concentrating, waiting for instructions. While the older boys discuss what to do next, Théo pours himself another glass and downs it as quickly as the first. No one says anything.

Now Baptiste explains the rules of the game. He'll ask each of them a question and then draw a card. For example, red or black? Spades, clubs, hearts or diamonds? If they answer correctly, he'll take a drink. If it's wrong, the other boy will. Then he'll move on to the next person and do the same again. And so on, clockwise round the circle.

They nod. They're ready. They're used to him telling them what to do.

An expectant silence.

Then Théo interjects: he'd like to ask the questions.

He hasn't challenged Baptiste's superiority or his entitlement. He didn't say 'I want to', just 'I'd like to'. He's the child of the separation of property and persons, of resentment, irreparable debts and child support: he knows how diplomacy works.

Heads turn towards Baptiste, who smiles, amused.

Quentin grins.

Baptiste sizes him up for a few seconds. Evaluates the transgressor. No sign of insurrection. Just a little boy's silly idea.

'You? You want to ask the questions? You do realise that under my rules, if you're in charge, you might have to drink five times as much as everyone else?'

'Yes, I know. I worked that out.'

'OK, I get it. You're good at maths ... You think you can hold your drink?'

They look at each other again. There's a hint of mockery, but a challenge is surfacing already. Baptiste hesitates to take him at his word. Théo sees all this but doesn't care what they think.

Baptiste has one last glance at his friends, then says, 'Go on then.'

He pushes the bottles across to Théo. They're different colours – orange, green, yellow – depending on what drink the alcohol's mixed with. Théo lines them up in front of him. The sugar has leaked out and the plastic is a bit sticky.

Baptiste finishes explaining: Théo must vary the questions he asks – face card or pips? Higher or lower than the previous one? Inside or outside the last two cards? Each type of question corresponds to the number of mouthfuls to be drunk, up to a maximum of four.

Quentin and Clément nudge each other as Baptiste gives the cards a final shuffle.

Théo takes the packet and asks the first question.

He loses. He drinks.

He asks another question. Loses again. And drinks.

The shrill sound in his head begins to fade.

He follows the rules. A gentle wave runs down his spine and his limbs feel softer, lifted or carried by a sort of light, smooth cotton wool.

He knows when he has to drink or hand over the bottle.

Laughter punctuates each challenge. But he knows that inside him something – some wave or flow – is escaping. He isn't afraid. He feels his muscles relax one by one: legs, arms, feet, fingers. Even his heart seems to slow, then slow still more. Everything has become fluid. Dilated.

He sees a huge white sheet dancing and flapping in the wind. The sun's come out again. He thinks he recognises his grandmother's washing line behind her old stone house.

He hears more laughter, but it isn't them. It's a higher note. Crystal, sharp, joyous.

MATHIS

Théo had put the two cards down in front of him, the ten of clubs and the queen of diamonds, face up. He turned to Quentin and asked, 'Inside or outside?'

Tiny flakes of snow had started dancing around them, but none of them seemed to be landing on the ground. Quentin closed his eyes before he answered.

'Inside.'

Théo turned over the card he held face down in his hand. Jack of spades.

Théo took the bottle and drank the four mouthfuls the rules demanded. Then suddenly fell backwards. He made a dull thud as he hit the ground.

They looked at each other. Quentin and Clément started laughing, but Baptiste said, 'Shut it!'

They straightened his legs. His upper body was lying on a carpet of leaves and his lower half on concrete. Baptiste gave him a few little slaps. He kept saying, 'Hey, hey, stop messing around!' but Théo didn't move. Mathis had never seen a body like that, so floppy.

The silence around them felt unreal. The whole city seemed to have obeyed Baptiste and come to a standstill.

Mathis would have sworn he could hear his heart thumping, a metronome like Mr Châle's, measuring these seconds of terror one by one. The smell of earth and rotting leaves caught his throat.

They looked at each other again. Hugo couldn't help himself giving a little groan of fear.

Baptiste gave the order: 'Leg it!'

He grabbed his brother's collar, stood him in front of him and held him fiercely by the shoulders. He looked him straight in the eye and said, 'We never came here, right?'

He turned to Mathis and repeated, 'We were never here, OK?'

Mathis nodded. The cold was cutting through his clothes.

In less than a minute, they've gathered everything up – cards, cigarettes, bottles – and disappeared.

Mathis stays behind, by his friend, who looks like he's in a deep sleep. He gets closer to his face and thinks he can see his breath.

He shakes him several times but Théo doesn't respond.

Mathis starts crying.

If he calls his mother, he'll have to admit that he's not at the Philharmonic. He lied and betrayed her trust.

She'll go crazy. And worst of all, she'll tell Théo's parents. And if someone goes to his father's place, Théo will be angry with him for the rest of his life.

Jumbled, obscure data he can't decode spins round in his head at high speed, an avalanche of threats he doesn't know how to put in order.

All his limbs are shaking and his teeth have begun to chatter, like those times he stays in the swimming pool too long.

It's time for him to go home. He must go home.

He calls, 'Théo!' And again. He shakes him, begs him. He tries one last time; his voice has become almost inaudible.

He puts his Puffa jacket on the outstretched body. Then leaves the gardens.

He takes avenue de La Motte-Picquet then the rue de Grenelle. He checks the time again and starts to run.

A few minutes later, he's outside his building. He taps in the entry code and goes into the lobby. He waits for a few seconds, long enough for his breathing to calm down. He puts his key in the door and instantly hears his mother's footsteps. She was waiting for him in the living room. She opens her arms in greeting.

She says, 'You're frozen.'

He snuggles against her. She strokes his hair and says, 'Don't worry. It's all going to be OK.' She doesn't ask him how the concert was. She probably thinks he's too tired and he'll tell her tomorrow.

In his room Mathis opens the cupboard where his clothes normally are.

It's empty.

He looks inside it several times.

Under the sheets, he tries to close his eyes. But images rush into his head, multiplying and dividing, operated by the turn of some invisible kaleidoscope. The colours get brighter and brighter and suddenly the exploded images all come together and appear to him whole. Perfectly clear.

The drawings from Ms Destrée's class loom up before his eyes, even when he keeps them open: a heart filled with blood whose rhythm is slowing, and then lungs frozen in ice, held in a film of frost, and then blood flowing on his hands, blue.

He sits up in bed; a silent sob tears at his chest.

And then he remembers that Ms Destrée gave them her number on the day of the trip to the Natural History Museum and asked every student to save it.

HÉLÈNE

It was almost midnight when my phone rang. A number I didn't recognise. I was about to put the light out. I hesitated before answering, but I picked up.

I heard rapid breathing, almost breathless. I almost hung up but I felt as though someone on the other end of the line was struggling not to cry. I waited and said nothing.

After a few seconds, a child's voice. He was ringing secretly; every word trembled and threatened to break down in sobs.

'Hello Miss. It's Mathis Guillaume. I wanted to tell you that Théo has passed out in Santiago du Chili gardens. He's on his own. Lying on the ground. Right at the back. He's had a lot to drink.'

I asked him to repeat the important information. How much to drink? How long ago? I pulled on my jeans, grabbed my jacket and left.

In the taxi I called an ambulance. I repeated what Mathis had told me word for word.

The taxi stopped right at the entrance to the gardens. I rushed to climb over the gate. I had set off into the darkness when the taxi driver called to me.

'Hey! Wait! Take this!'

The wind was puffing up the survival blanket. It seemed to be giving off a light of its own.

Note on the Author

Delphine de Vigan is the prize-winning author of bestselling *No and Me*, which was a Richard & Judy selection in Britain, *Nothing Holds Back the Night*, *Underground Time* and *Based on a True Story*. She lives in Paris.

Note on the Translator

George Miller is the translator into English of all four of Delphine de Vigan's previous titles. He is also a regular translator for *Le Monde diplomatique*'s English-language edition.